MW01146879

Breaking

DRAGON

SAVAGE BROTHERS MC SERIES
BOOK 1

Jordan Marie

Copyright © 2014-16

All rights reserved. No part of this publication may be reproduced, distributed, or transmitted in any form or by any means, including photocopying, recording, or other electronic or mechanical methods, without the prior written permission of the author.

WARNING: The unauthorized reproduction or distribution of this copyrighted work is illegal. No part of this book may be scanned, uploaded or distributed via the internet or any other means, electronic or print, without the publisher's/author's permission. Criminal copyright infringement, including infringement without monetary gain, is investigated by the FBI and is punishable by up to 5 years in federal prison and a fine of 250,000.00 (http://www.fbi.gov/ipr/). Please purchase only authorized electronic or print editions and do not participate or encourage the electronic piracy of copyrighted material. Your respect of the author's rights is appreciated.

This book is a work of fiction and any resemblance to persons, living or dead, or places events or locales is purely coincidental. The characters are created from the author's imagination and used in a fictitious manner. While some places in this book might mention actual areas or places, author acknowledges that it was purely for entertainment purposes and not endorsed by owners or has nothing to do with actual place and was mentioned to further reader's enjoyment only.

Cover by Rebel Edit Designs

www.rebeleditdesign.com

Margreet Asselbergs

Cover image purchased through Erotic Stock Photos

eroticstockphotos.com

Big Stock Photos

www.bigstockphoto.com

Re-Edit & Interior Formatting by Daryl Banner

www.darylbanner.com

Trademarks: Any brands, titles, artists used in this book were mentioned purely for artistic purposes and are either used as a product of the author's imagination or used fictitiously. None of the herein mentioned products, artists etc., endorse this book whatsoever and the author acknowledges their trademarked status which has been used in this work of fiction. Author acknowledges trademarked status or owners of various products and further acknowledges that said use is not authorized or endorsed by said owners.

This e-book is licensed for your personal enjoyment only. It is not to be re-sold or given away to others and doing so is a violation of the copyright.

Warning: The content in this book is for mature audiences only. Contains sexual situations and violence, reader should please read with that knowledge.

Table of Contents

DEDICATION

To everyone who took a chance on an unknown author
thank you from the bottom of my heart and to my badass crew
you make each day better #BB4L

xoxo

J

Breaking DRAGON

Nicole

It's Sunday, and that in itself shouldn't be a momentous thing because you get one of those every week, if you're lucky enough to survive. Still it is, because today is the day that Dani and I are picking up the last of our boxes and moving out of Blade. Blade, Kentucky is a small hole in the wall with less than one hundred people living there. Bet you didn't know places like that existed, did you? Well they do. We have a city hall, one bank, a gas station/tobacco store, and a volunteer fire department. That's the grand total of all the buildings in Blade. The few kids who live here are driven by their parents to a school one county over. I've lived here my entire life and even though it may sound like it, I'm not really complaining. I love Blade. It's living with my parents that I don't enjoy.

My parents really shouldn't have settled down here. After all, there are no country clubs, no private dining facilities and none of the amenities befitting their station. Yes, that is sarcasm you detect. I've heard those words a million times coming from my mother's lips, those same lips that had never kissed the top of my head when I was sad, nor spoke words of encouragement when I failed. Lips that have been painted deep ruby red for as long as I could remember, and brought to mind a cold and lifeless corpse.

You might be realizing there is no love lost between my mother and me—you would be right. The simple truth is my

1

parents remain in Blade because my dad, Marcus Samuel Wentworth the second, owns the sole bank in the city and the one in the neighboring area of Burkesville. Here, my parents are important, specifically my mother. If she moved away, she would lose that distinction, and Gwyneth couldn't handle that. My father would too for that matter, as he was a step or two up from mother dear, but that's not really saying much. Sometimes, I wonder how I could be their daughter. I would have thought I was adopted except for my hair. The dirty-blonde hair I have is the same color as my mother's. For that reason alone, I put a darker caramel color through it, so now it looks nothing like hers. She hated it. I celebrated it.

I'm getting all dragged down talking about the parental units. That's enough to depress me and that can't happen on this awesome day. Today, Dani and I are moving to London, Kentucky. See? Momentous!

Okay, well it isn't that far from here to be honest, but it is at least a three hour drive and that's good for now. We rented a two bedroom house on the outskirts of the city and it'll be far enough away from my parents. Dani and I both have jobs. I'm going to be a waitress at the Wolves Den and she will be dancing. I'd never have the nerve to dance for several reasons. First, Dani makes me brave, but she can't make me believe I don't have mega flaws. Dani is drop dead gorgeous. Me? That's reason number two. I have boobs that are a little too large, and my ass is just a tad too wide. My thighs aren't my favorite thing either. I'm a size fourteen. I'll never fit into Dani's size eights. I used to want to, but as I got older I decided I like who I am well enough. So screw it. Plus, I'm pretty outspoken at times, but way too freaking shy to be a dancer. My girl makes me brave, but there isn't anyone able to make me brave enough to bare my boobs and ass to a bunch of strangers. It's going to be hard enough getting used to wearing the mini booty shorts and black tank uniform that shows way too much of the aforementioned boobs, but I'm determined.

I want to branch out into real life and live. So I've made the decision to not let my conscience get the better of me and just experience the different things that are out there. It's silly, and a decision that may bite me in the ass.

I've never really been the type to want to go to college. That's an issue my parents bring up regularly—just another thing on a long list of my failures. I've never really had aspirations to do something with my life other than enjoy it. Maybe I'll make plans later on. I don't know what yet and frankly at twenty-four I probably should, but I don't really care right now. It took too long to break away from Blade. I'll figure it out as I go along.

"Woo!!!!!!!!" Dani hollers as we're speeding down the interstate in my Mercedes.

Her hands are waving in the air and I can't help but laugh over the pounding of the radio. I love my car. It's a shit hot baby blue Mercedes E350 Convertible, and it's the only thing my parents gave me that I love. It's the last gift they ever gave me. It was when I was graduating from high school and they still thought they had a chance of molding me into who they thought I should be. Luckily, it was in my name and paid for when they gave me the keys. One month later, they found out I wouldn't be going to college to find myself a future doctor or lawyer as a husband. Yes, that was the reason given for why I should enroll in college. I refused, and then I was pretty much cut off. Luckily, I had Dani. She had always been there for me. We were as different as night and day and honestly, there is no *reason* why Dani and I are friends. Some things just happen. Dani walks to the beat of her own drum. She is a force of nature, a hurricane— or rather, more like a category five hurricane. She inspires me. She scares me. She makes me happy and I love her. She took me in and I lived with her and her brother Roy, who was a nice guy and cute as hell. Too bad he was also gay. That was just my luck.

We did okay there, working to save every bit of money we could until we had enough to make a big move. Three hours away might not be a big move for some, but it sure as hell was for us. We pooled our money and were able to pay the rent for three months, plus the safety deposit. We had enough left over to fully stock the fridge and pay utilities until we got paid from our new jobs. Roy had a friend who worked as a manager at Wolves Den and got us interviews. We nailed the jobs and told them we needed two weeks to give our former employers notice. We didn't really, but it takes time to move and get settled. It happened so quickly once we made the decision, that my head is still kind of dizzy, but I'm happy. I looked over at my best friend for life and smiled—really happy.

"Hey, I'm thirsty!" Dani hollered.

"We're just thirty minutes or so away!" I yelled back, not crazy about stopping.

"Big damn deal. Let's get some drinks and chocolate, girl!" She yelled back.

I frowned and looked down at my gas gauge. I could use some gas. I put on my turn signal to get over and took the upcoming exit. We had to take it anyway to get to where our new home would be, so off I go. We pulled into the first gas station I saw and I cut the engine off, pushing my hands through my hair and shaking it out, because hello, interstate driving, convertible. Enough said.

"Whatcha' want bitch?" Dani asked, and I shake my head at her. She's yelling over the music. Ludacris is blasting through the speakers.

"Pepsi, fountain if they have it," I yell back, looking around. I notice there's a bunch of men on bikes by the entrance, and they're looking over at us laughing as I open the door, cutting off Ludacris as he screams out about his woman riding his dick. I can feel the heat rising up in my face and turn my eyes from them immediately. Shit!

Our "on the road" play list is very eclectic and the Ludacris' offering is one of Dani's choices. Don't get me wrong, I like it. I like a bit of naughty and I like the beat, but it's not my usual thing. Lorde's Team is next. That's me, but what the hell. I don't know the men who are laughing, maybe they aren't even laughing at me. It felt like they were though. I hate this about me. I am so self-conscious I automatically take things personally and find myself lacking. Dani isn't like that. She'd flip the bikers off and go about her business. I wanted to be more carefree like Dani; I just could never achieve it. They are laughing harder now, but I turn around to the pump and run my card through and ignore them. In my mind I'm wondering if my ass is hanging out of my cut-offs and if that's why they are laughing. Can they see the small catsup stain on my pink shirt from the fries we had shared in the car earlier? I set the pump to go on its own and start cleaning the trash out of the car. I'm mostly trying to keep myself busy and ignoring the bikers. It takes a while and my conclusion is that my girl and I are pigs.

I walk over to the garbage can and am throwing away all the crap when a deep gravelly voice from behind me sends chills up my back.

"Damn. I've heard of it, but I don't think I've ever seen it." I turn slowly and look up to see one of the bikers standing in front of me. I bite my lip and move back a small step. I grind my teeth into one corner of my bottom lip and my hands go to the back pockets of my shorts as I take him in, and damn there is a lot to take in. Holy Mother of God, standing before me is a man that towers over me. He's at least a good six feet tall. His mocha skin glistens in the sun and he's wearing a black t-shirt that's faded to the point it's almost gray, over which he has on a leather vest. Weird, because it's like eighty freaking degrees today, but I can't deny he looks sexy. I think maybe he could wear a feed sack and it'd be sexy.

The vest has the word Savage written on it in dark red letters, on top of what looks like a rabid wolf. It's kind of scary looking. Underneath that is the word "President". I move my eyes up from his massive chest and the biceps covered in tattoos, to look into the most gorgeous eyes I have ever seen in my life. They are a deep, dark, sparkling brown, and I think I could drown in them and be happy. His hair is cut short to his head with just enough left that you can still feel the texture against your skin.

I let go of my lips and lick them because my whole mouth has gone dry.

The god before me would be a good way to let go and experience life, Bad Nicole whispers in my head, and the sane part of me agrees. I wouldn't mind a piece of what stands before me, not that I'd ever have a chance of holding onto him, but still.

"What's that?" I ask and shit does my voice sound breathless.

"A barefoot Kentucky girl." he says.

I look down at my feet, realizing I left my flip flops in the car. I hate shoes and I absolutely hate driving with shoes on. I tend to wrap my toes around the pedals of a car and you can't do that with shoes on. I forget to put them back on all the time. I once went to the grocery store and got all the way to the door, before I noticed I was barefoot.

I look back at him and turn my head to the side in what I hoped was a flirty action.

"You must be new to Kentucky." I'm feeling warm all over. Can he see the heat rising on my face?

"No Mama. Been here awhile and seen a lot of girls, in a lot of places. Don't believe I've ever seen one pumping gas barefoot."

"Glad I could be your first," I grin, wondering if he could pick up on the sexual innuendo. I'm subtle, way too subtle sometimes, as Dani likes to remind me constantly.

His lush, full lips widen into a smile and his bright white teeth are visible for a minute. It's a good smile. Damn good.

"What's your name Twinkie?" he asks. The boys with him laugh harder. I don't know why, maybe it was just a sixth sense, but I don't think I like that name. Now, when he had called me Mama? I'm pretty sure I drenched my panties.

"Does it matter?" I ask, a little confused with the situation coming at me.

"I like to know the name of the woman who took my virginity," he quipped, his long arm leaning against the post by the gas pump.

Guess that means he picked up on my innuendo. Only now with his boys laughing, I get the feeling this was some kind of game, and that disappointed me. I have been the butt of too many jokes, way too often, mostly because of my size.

The pump kicked off and I reached down to take the nozzle out when he did it for me. His hand brushed mine. I felt a charge of electricity at that small touch and my nipples harden in reaction. Damn, that had never happened before and this guy was the wrong person for it to be happening with.

"How about you just call me mystery, that way you won't get me confused with the millions of girls that come after me," I smiled, though it probably didn't reach my eyes, but he wouldn't know that.

"Damn Nic, when I said I wanted chocolate, you didn't have to go all out bitch. Hello there Tall Dark and Do me all over," Dani piped up as I closed the gas lid and shook my head.

I turn back around to see him look Dani up and down and I don't miss the interest flair in his eyes. I sigh, yep, no competing with Dani. I take my pop from her hand while she is still staring at Stud Muffin.

"Dani meet Stud, Stud meet Dani. I popped his cherry while you were in the store," I say walking around to the driver's side of the car. The men laugh harder as I continue to ignore them. Dani laughs and opens the door, careful not to hit him as she gets in and I notice he closes her door. Damn. Yeah, that's jealousy I feel. Dang it! Stud doesn't move away either. His hands are firmly propped on the passenger door and he leans in the window. Damn Dani and her sexy size eights. Still, when I look up, his eyes are on me.

"Me and my crew," he said, and jerks his head in the

direction of the men who had finally stopped laughing, "are having a party this Tuesday. You girls should come. It's the least you can do for stealing my virginity and all Nicole. I was saving that," he said, stressing my name to let me know he had it now.

"Sorry Stud, we just moved and have some stuff to do before we start work Friday," I reply, starting up the car. Immediately, Ludacris fills the air again, but I reach down and mute it quickly.

"Where are you working?" he asks, looking straight at me, and I wonder if for a minute I mistook his interest in Dani, but then I realize he's sizing us both up. He's a player, a total player—disappointing, but not surprising.

"Wolves Den," I say putting the car in drive, but I keep my foot on the brake. His smile grows and he walks around the front of the car and slaps the hood.

"Maybe I'll see you around sometime then Twinkie."

"Sorry, I don't do repeats, it's hard to beat that first time," I reply waiting for him to move past the hood so I can go on.

"Now that's damned disappointing. Maybe I can show you how some things get better with practice," he purrs.

"It's nice you believe in miracles. Good to know I didn't take all your innocence," I return. He barely clears my car before I give it some gas and pull out from the pumps, intent on getting away.

"Be seeing you soon!" he calls out.

I ignore the warning and the chills it sends down my spine, and turn the sound back up on my radio. By this time Creep from Radiohead, is on so I crank it high.

"Who the hell was that?" Dani asks when we get on the road, turning my music back down.

"Have no idea. Thought he was sexy, but he seemed to be getting his jollies off messing with me, while his buddies laughed."

Dani was silent, but I saw her nod out of the corner of my eye.

We went down the road about a mile or so before I noticed the bikes behind us. I could see Stud in my rearview mirror, his shades covering his eyes. Damn he was sex on a stick.

"Don't look now, but I think your play toy is following you," Dani said looking through her side mirror. I turned on the signal to cut down road 80, where the house we had rented was located. I couldn't help but notice the bikes followed.

"Do you think we should be worried?" I ask, trying not to hyperventilate.

"Nah, it's a long road, maybe they live on it, or maybe he just wants to tap your ass. Worse things could happen girl. Hell, it's been forever since you got laid."

She wasn't wrong. I had been with two other guys. One was in high school. I was sixteen and gave my virginity to my boyfriend Marshall after prom. Both Marshall and the giving away of my virginity were a mistake. The second was the last relationship I was in, with Tony or as I affectionately referred to him, Tony the Tool. I sucked the big one at picking men.

We drove a little further along the road then turn up a dirt road on the right that leads to the house we rented. We'd found it in an ad online and rented it just by the pictures. Apparently the pictures were old because the grass out front looked like it would come up past my knees. Holy Splendor in the Grass, Batman!

"Shit," Dani said, and I wholeheartedly agreed as we pulled into the drive. I parked and we got out, still in shock.

We hear the bikes following us in and somehow I wasn't surprised, but I was still in shock over the house, so my attention was somewhat diverted. I was counting up the hours I'd be stuck doing yard work and praying the house was in better shape, when Tall, dark and studly parked his bike beside me.

"Nice place, Twinkie," he said and at least this time the boys weren't laughing.

I turned so I could face him. God he was hot. Did I forget to mention that? Even if I didn't, it sure as hell needs repeating.

"Listen, it's cute how you cling to me and everything, but first rule in 'Cherry Popping 101' is: hit it and quit it. So really we should say goodbye now." I hear Dani snort over his men's laughter.

"You go barefoot in these weeds Mama and you're liable to get snake bit."

I roll my eyes. "I have shoes, plus last time I checked I was a big girl, so you don't need to worry Daddy." I open the car door, get out my flip flops and put them on my feet.

I was giving him much more lip than I normally would. I wasn't sure why, but I think it was because it felt like he and his men were laughing at me earlier. If you added that along with the fact he checked out Dani, who I could never compete with, while I was standing right there.....

"I've never liked that before," he said resignedly, getting off his bike.

I take a step back now that he is standing beside me. I had to move away to try and get air or I would have swooned. It was a near miss as it was.

"What's that?" I ask, suddenly lost to the conversation.

"Being called Daddy, but it might be hot as hell from you.

Especially, if you scream it out while I'm spanking that ass of yours."

Have you ever seen a goldfish jump out of its bowl and flap around? Its mouth opening and closing while it's trying desperately to breathe? I'm pretty sure that's what I looked like.

Then he shocked me further by picking me up and walking me towards the house.

"Wait! What on earth are you doing?"

"Mama those things on your feet are cute as hell, but they aren't going to protect you from snakes." I hear Dani laughing and looked over Stud's shoulders to see her piggy back riding one of the other men. She was having the time of her life, while I was confused, aroused and panicked. See? Totally different from Dani, damn it!

"Put me down! I'm too heavy," I say, feeling way out of my depth here. I had never been literally picked up by a man before, but especially by a man I didn't even know. At my words, he shifts and turns me so I am hanging half over his back. His hand comes up and slaps me hard on the ass.

"Ow! What the hell was that for?"

"Quit talking about yourself like that. You sure as hell aren't heavy."

"I don't even know you, you creep. What the hell do you think you're doing?"

"Spanking an ass I plan on tapping later?" *Gulp!* I think this might be an Oh-shit-moment if ever there was one. What do you say to that? I mean I didn't even know him!

JUMP HIM! Bad Nicole orders in my head. She seems to be coming out to play more and more around this man, and I only met him thirty minutes ago! If that!

"There's no way in hell!" I growl, as he puts me down on the small cement square in front of the back door.

Liar! Bad Nicole chided.

I really need to find a way to slap that bitch.

"Oh yeah there is Mama, and something else you should know, before I'm through you're going to be begging me to spank you harder."

My face jerks back like he had hit me. Seriously? Did he just say that to me? I would have argued, but he picks that moment to grab me by the back of the head and pull me to him. My hands come up between us, to try and pull away. He is too strong, or maybe I didn't really try. He slams his lips against mine and slides his mouth over mine possessively. I grind my teeth together refusing to open for him. His tongue teases along the inside of my bottom lip. It feels good. It feels divine, yet somehow I had the wherewithal to not open my mouth.

Because you're stupid! Bad Nicole should seriously go back into hibernation.

Stud must have gotten impatient because I can feel his hand moving between us. It leaves a heated path through my shirt along my stomach, and his touch is gentle, but oh so commanding. I would be lying if I didn't admit my resistance is melting. It so was, but in the end that didn't matter. His hand reaches up to my chest and he places that big, warm palm over my right breast. Moisture begins pooling in my panties and I can feel heat moving through my body and centering on all the pleasure receptors in my body. I am preparing to have them blown sky high when he twists my nipple between his fingers. The jolt of pain was so intense, it made me gasp. It's just the opening he wanted. He pushes his tongue in my mouth, finding mine and teasing it, drawing it out to play with his. I am helpless to stop it. A woman would have to be dead not to respond to this man's kiss. Our tongues dance and tangle. I can't stop my moan that releases into his mouth. It's a mere vibration, barely a whisper of a sound, but it gives him all the encouragement he needs. I know that by the way his thumb brushes over the erect nipple he had inflicted pain on earlier. My arms circle around his neck as my body pushes in. I need to get closer to him.

I push my fingers into his hair, the texture abrasive and exactly as I imagined. I'm trying to get his mouth closer, even though that is physically impossible. I want to devour him. The kiss turns up another notch, hell another ten notches. His hands move down to my ass cupping it, kneading it and bringing me up his body. His hard cock pushes where I need it most. I'm not sure what would have happened next. I think I might have let him fuck me right there on the porch. I was that ready, that needy, that willing to go there. Until the hoots and hollers from his friends start, my body locks and I pull away, regretfully. I look into his warm dark chocolate eyes, and I have to catch my breath at the beauty.

His fingers bite into my ass. I realized I was squeezing my thighs into the side of his like a wanton hussy, but seriously that's what he's turned me into. I might as well own it. I push against his shoulders and release my legs so he would put me down. Luckily, Bad Nicole is as speechless as I am.

Stud watches me and somehow his eyes get darker. Oh they looked good before, but now I melt, and from the sticky wetness between my legs I could honestly say I mean that literally.

I tear my eyes away from him and look down at his feet. I feel heat enter my cheeks as the men with him keep ragging at us. He lowers me back to the ground slowly, my heart pounding, beating hard and echoing in my ears.

I step back the minute my feet hit concrete. My fingers come up to my swollen lips, as the world begins to right itself. In the background I can hear the boys making comments. I'm sure it would embarrass me to death, but I can't concentrate. I glance at him and then try to look away, but can't seem to pull my eyes off of his face.

"You should come by the club tonight Twinkie. Me and the boys are just right up the road. We could show you and your girl a real good time."

I blinked. My brain was addled. We? He didn't mean that the way it sounded. Right?

"The club?" I ask confused, trying to focus my thoughts, but that was easier said than done.

"Yeah babe, me and the boys are the Savage MC. Our clubhouse is up the road about fifteen miles. Just take a left by the old barn and follow the road till it veers left…not that hard to find. We're always looking for new Twinkies. You and your girl would fit right in. I'll even make sure you enjoy it personally," he said twirling my hair around his finger.

"I…you…." I stopped. I had been looking forward to this man blowing my mind, but I just didn't think it would be like that. Damn him for telling me this! It makes me feel raw inside and it hurts. I can feel embarrassment flooding through me. I hadn't been exposed to that kind of thing, but I do read romance novels. I loved reading Motorcycle Club erotica even. What girl didn't? In my books, I had heard club women referred to as muffler bunnies, mattress monkeys, sweet butts, candy, club toys, and a million other things. They all rounded down to one word. Whore! I had never heard the word "Twinkies" used, but I could imagine it was one in the same.

"We could make all your hot little wicked fantasies come true baby…every last fucking one, no matter how filthy," he leans down and whispers in my ear.

I pull away from him like his touch burns, and damn it all to hell it did!

After three steps back I look around to see his men in the background behind my car all smiling, leering and joking. I see Dani get away from the guy who had given her a ride. She walks behind me and Stud with a strange look on her face. She takes the key we had been mailed, opens the door and stands there waiting.

"What makes you think we're looking to be Twinkies?" I ask evenly. I was proud of myself because you couldn't hear the hurt in my voice.

"C'mon babe, no one lights up in a man's arms as quick as you do unless she's hot for it. No shame babe. You want to piss off your rich ass parents? You won't be the first. Just so happens, this time I happen to like the idea of helping you make that goal."

He sounds so cocky and looks so sure of himself. How could I have forgotten my earlier thoughts? Player…total player.

"Sorry to disappoint you Stud, but it hasn't been my life's dream to be a Savage chew toy. Also, I ceased to care what my parents thought of me a couple of years ago, when I pissed them off for the last time. You should run home now, I'm sure you have…Twinkies was it? Twinkies there to take care of all your wicked little fantasies!"

With that I turn around. I thought it was a good line. I am proud of myself. I can tell by Dani's smile she was too. But Stud, won't let it pass. He grabs my hand to pull me back around.

"You can't deny what you were offering Mama. A man can only go by what you put out there."

I take a deep breath. I pull my hand so he gets the message to let me go. He does, but he gives me a look that makes it plain he isn't about to leave until we have this, whatever this was, out.

"First of all, if I remember correctly you started calling me Twinkie before I offered you jack shit. In fact, I don't believe I have yet to offer you anything Stud. So please stop wasting my time and yours. Run along," I say making a movement with my hand like I was scurrying away a dog. Heck, he is most assuredly a dog.

"Babe, that kiss you sure as hell offered, and you were definitely sending out those vibes earlier."

"Oh my God! I was flirting! Women do that when they think someone standing before them is hot!" He grins, and I swear at that moment I want to slap the shit out of him. How could someone you just met make you feel such a range of emotions?

"And besides that," I continue, before I gave in to the urge to kill him, "it was just a damn kiss." I hold up my hand when he starts to argue with me. "It was a fucking kiss, nothing else! I don't even know your name for God sake!"

I turn to the door when his voice stops me, "Dragon."

"What?" I ask, looking over my shoulder.

"My name is Dragon."

"I seriously doubt that, but in either case it doesn't matter as I won't be using it."

"Learn it Mama. Trust me, you will be fucking screaming it out and soon."

I ignore him. I mean really, what can you say after that…especially when my body wanted to agree with him. I make it inside the kitchen and slam the door. I lean against it and look at Dani. We stare at each other a minute and then Dani grins.

"So, that was interesting," she deadpans.

I look at her like she had just grown three heads. We hear the bikes start up outside and then slowly we both start laughing, as I sink to the floor on my ass.

Dragon

My boys and I pull into the club and I don't talk. They're still laughing their asses off, and hell I would be too if it had happened to Crusher or one of the other men.

I stomp into the club, go to the bar and looking over at the prospect, I bark out "Jack!"

He nods, puts a glass in front of me and pours it in.

"Leave the bottle."

He does as told, and goes back to wiping the glasses he's stocking on the shelves behind the bar.

Crusher, my VP and best friend, saddles up on the stool beside me. He doesn't talk. I know he is dying to say something. Crusher and I had been through some tough shit. He has always had my back and though I trust all of my brothers, Crusher is someone special to me. We had forged a bond in blood. It would stand till the world stopped.

"She's a hot little piece," Crusher says, as the prospect puts a glass down in front of him. He grabs my bottle and pours himself a drink. Bastard!

I grunt, finishing off my drink and pouring another one. My mind keeps flashing back to that kiss. That damn fucking kiss and how it felt to have my hands full of that thick ass. I'm still hard thinking about her. I have screwed the pooch with the way I handled things. I wasn't about to let go till I got my taste though, that was just fact. She's not anything I ever thought of nailing to be honest. I mean she is sexy as fuck, but I never went for the rich bitches. Hell, I never went for any kind really. I nailed the pussy at the club and let it go. My life was too fucked up to think about attaching myself to one woman, and I sure as hell wasn't the type to date. I was thirty-six years old, have never been on a fucking date, never imagined going on one and I never would. In my life, you were lucky to be alive and survive, that's the way it has always been and appeared to be how life was made for me. Miss Nicole's fucking shoes probably cost more than my bike. Not that it really bothers me. The club makes sure we all have a good fucking life as far as money goes, but I sure wasn't into that high-brow shit. In fact, it'd be best if I forget the bitch exists, except when I saw her standing at the gas station barefoot, with that luscious round ass barely contained in her cut-off jeans and those damned tits looking so juicy, I had to get closer and that hasn't changed.

When she started driving towards the club? I couldn't help myself. I had to check her out further. The last thing I expected was the punch that kiss had delivered. I could still taste her on my lips and fuck me, I wanted a deeper taste.

"You gonna push it?" I knew what Crusher was asking. What I didn't know was the answer.

"Fuck if I know," I answer honestly.

"Let me know if you don't," he says evenly. I look up at him.

"Hey man. She's damned fine."

"She's got trouble written all over her." I'm not feeling his interest at-fucking-all.

"Yeah, but what a trip. Some things are worth the trouble man. She caught on fire for you. I'd like to see how deep that fire runs."

I want to slam my fist in his head. How fucked up is that? Fuck yeah, she had caught on fire. I was the lucky bastard who got to feel it. I was damned glad he hadn't or I might have been forced to kill him.

"Hey Dragon, you looking for some company?" Tash asks, coming up behind me and hanging on my back.

Tash is a club whore and I have used her a few times. She was clean and knew how to ride a man's cock, which was about the only requirement of club Twinkies. She wasn't much to look at in the face and her body was too damned boney to suit me, but she was tight. I smile thinking about Nicole. The little spitfire didn't like the idea of being club pussy and I like the sass she showed.

"Nah, Tash why don't you see to my brother here. I got things on my mind girl." I watch as Crusher's eyebrow shoots up. He knew what the fuck I was doing. I wanted him to tire himself out so he'd quit thinking about Nicole. He laughs and the sound grates on my nerves. Tash walks over and slams her lips down on Crusher's. Crusher took the kiss and moved his hand up under the barely there mini dress she had on, pushing it up so her naked ass was hanging out. Easy access was a must for club whores, most of our men didn't like waiting for it.

Crusher stands up slapping my shoulder. "She starts work next week at the club man. Let me know before then or she's fair game."

Bastard!

I take a breath, turn and look out over my club and men. We are a fucking rag tag bunch. Crusher, Irish, Gunner, Bull, Freak, Dancer and myself made up the seven original members of

Savage Brothers. We are all brothers, having grown up on the streets and sifting through the system. We learned to depend on no one but ourselves and now our brothers. We brought in Twist and Striker, a move I was beginning to think might bite us in the ass. I still wasn't sure how I felt about either of them.

We had been low on members when Dancer got sent to the big house. He shot and killed a man who had been trying to rape some chick in an alley. Unfortunately for Dancer, it had been in a county we didn't own and the son of a bitch turned out to be the sheriff's brother. Prosecution made it look like the girl had been a whore, maybe she was, but I didn't know. I heard she was living a couple of counties over working at a department store. I did know my brother got a raw ass deal. He was currently serving out a fifteen year sentence. We had a club lawyer working on an appeal since the other man had been holding a knife on the girl and came after Dancer with it, and I was hoping it worked. Dancer couldn't fucking stand being locked behind bars. I worried about him, and at my last visit something had been off. I'm afraid he is close to losing his shit.

We had four prospects right now and so far I wasn't particularly impressed. I fill my glass again, last time though. I need a clear head to figure out what the fuck is going on with me. How do you become obsessed with a woman you just met? Someone that was completely unlike anyone you had ever wanted before. Maybe all I need is to get laid and work out the tension.

There were two Twinkies dancing on the poles in the middle of the room. I don't even know their real names; we just call them the twins. They weren't in fact twins, though they both had fake tits, pitch black hair and milky white skin. Good looking women, but the best damn thing about them was they liked to tag team a man or men as the case was now. I watch them twist and turn and rub against each other as Frog, Hawk and Gunner start playing with them.

My dick doesn't even twitch. In fact, it seems to deflate from the semi hard-on I had left over from the Rich Bitch. Yeah, that was a better name for her. It reminds me of why I shouldn't have a damn thing to do with her.

My attention turns to Lips, a mocha-skinned, hot little minx with an ass that was fucking fantastic. I knew exactly how that ass felt wrapped around my dick too and bonus, Lips was a screamer. She sees me staring at her and I enjoy watching the way her breasts bounce under that white t-shirt she's wearing with only a black thong. I admit, she is one well put together woman. She wasn't like the other club whores either. She liked sex, lots of sex and made no apologies for it. I respected it in a way. Part of me always wondered about making her my old lady. Not because of any great connection, but sometimes I thought about settling down with a chick that was all mine. I shared from time to time and it was fucking hot to watch a woman pushed to her limits with two men. I fucking loved it. Still, that shit wasn't me in the long term. If a condom ever fucking let me down, I wanted to know whatever was planted in the woman was mine. Lately, I had been thinking more and more of that. I think if I did take an old lady I'd have to make sure she couldn't fucking have kids. I sure as hell didn't know what on Earth to do with them anyway.

"Hey baby. You look like you could use some loving tonight," Lips purrs, and slides up on my lap.

She grinds that round ass against my cock and he perks up

with interest. She bends down and kisses along the side of my neck. It feels good, really damn good. Just one problem, as hot as she was...she wasn't what was on my mind right now.

"Maybe later, got some shit to do right now," I said, kissing her shoulder to let her down gently.

"I'll hold you to that Dragon," she says regretfully, heading back to where the other boys were playing cards.

Tonight was going to be a quiet night. Club party nights were usually on Mondays and Tuesdays. We stayed busy with the clubs and other businesses the rest of the time. Today is Sunday and the MC owned clubs are closed. It is the middle of the day and there will probably be a small party here tonight, but I don't want to stay. Ever since the kiss with that little hot number, I was feeling antsy. I feel like I am crawling out of my skin. Would it be stalking if I went back down to her house? I mean, technically the club owns the house. Wasn't it my duty to see that she settles in okay?

I should have had a prospect clean the damn place up. I had forgotten Irish had rented it out to be honest. Maybe I'll take a few prospects with me tomorrow and get them to cut the grass and shit. That might help thaw out her ass. Why the fuck I want her thawed out I don't know, but I do just the same.

Dragon

It's around one in the afternoon the next day. Sad truth was I had barely waited till now to hunt Nicole down. I had actually meant to get started earlier but my fucking VP wouldn't let it alone. So here I am pulling up to Nicole's house with two prospects and Crusher. I don't want Crusher here, but the asshole wouldn't stay behind. I could have insisted, but fuck I wasn't ready to admit to myself why I didn't like it! I sure as hell wasn't ready to show anyone else how fucked up in the head I am about this girl.

The chick that was with Nicole yesterday is out on the front porch with her legs kicked out on the banister. Her hair was swept back in a ponytail and she looked good in her cotton shorts and tank top. She grins when she sees us. Too bad my dick wasn't interested in her. I had a feeling I'd make it in there a lot easier than I will with Nicole. Damn cock didn't even jerk though. For the most part it hadn't come to life at all last night, despite the promise of a night with Lips. If Nicole could do that to me after one kiss, what the hell would happen when I manage to get more?

"Well lookie here. What brings you boys back out our way?" the chick asks, bringing a coffee cup to her lips.

"Thought you girls could use some help cleaning this shit up," I answer trying to look around to see where Nicole is.

"Well that would be nice," she replies, watching me closely.

"Where's your girl?"

"One of the servers quit at the Den and they needed her to start today instead of Friday. She's working the lunch and dinner shift."

Shit. "Yo, Frog!" I yell. Frog comes up to stand beside me. "This here is Frog, he's due to be patched in next month. Anything you want done, Frog and the other two over there will do it."

I didn't give her a chance to reply. I went to my bike and hopped on. Unfortunately, I saw Crusher doing the same. Motherfucker!

"Hey, Dragon?"

I look up at the dark haired minx I knew was laughing at me, even if not right out in front of my face.

"Where are you headed?"

I ignore her, not bothering to answer. I just start my bike and the bitch actually laughs out loud. I flip her off and she laughs harder. I'm starting to like her. Go figure.

It takes thirty minutes for me and my boy to reach the Den. The bar hangs back on the Tennessee line and was the first Adult Club we opened up. During the day it is mostly a regular bar with food and drinks served. At night, we keep at least two dancers up on the bar where poles are installed. It does damn good business, and between it and the other three businesses Savage MC owns, the club has mostly gone legit. We still have our fingers in some shit though. I do that just to keep the bigger charter out of our territory and keep them further down in Georgia.

I know Nicole has no idea the club owns this place, or the house she rented. Hell, she was so clueless she probably doesn't realize the MC owns the whole damn town.

I walk in leaving Crusher to follow behind me. Irish is behind the bar. He jerks his head in greeting. I look around to see if I could spot Nicole and fuck me! There she is. I suddenly hate the outfits the waitresses wear. Shorts so damned tiny the globes of her ass hang out even more than the day before. She has a tight little black tank top that shows the sides of her tits. Fuck! A man could get hypnotized with the way they sway when she walks. I sit down at a table in the back and watch as Crusher slowly makes his way to me. Bastard, I should rename the asshole.

"Get your goddamned eyes back in your head before I knock them back in," I growl, when he eye fucks Nicole the minute he catches sight of her.

Crusher tears his eyes from her and looks at me. Then he laughs his ass off. Yep, Bastard is his new fucking name.

"Seem awful territorial there Prez."

Yeah so what? I thought, but didn't say out loud. I was too busy watching Nicole come over to our table. She stumbles when she sees me, but to her credit she keeps coming.

"Boys," she says. "You need a menu?"

"Two beers, house brand," I answer quietly, watching her. Her tongue darts out and her face takes on a light blush. She licks her lips and I nearly groan at the way my dick instantly springs up, demanding attention. She stares at me for a minute and then takes off back towards the bar. I get to her. The thought registers and satisfaction thrums through me. My body, which had been dead, is currently sporting a raging hard-on.

"I take it you're staking a claim?" Crusher says, and I can hear the disappointment in his voice. It pisses me off. Crusher is a good looking fucker, even I could admit that. If he pressed it though, would Nicole pick him over me? I was rough around the edges, while Crusher was smooth and easy going. Just the type a little rich girl would prefer.

I nod looking him straight in the eye, and daring him to argue. I am not about to give him the chance to move in. She doesn't have a choice. She's not going to have one. Nicole is mine. She just doesn't know it yet. Maybe I'd let Crusher have her when I am done. I totally ignore the sour taste that thought leaves in me.

"Pity."

"Are we going to have trouble over this shit?" I growl, watching the woman in question make her way through the room, towards our table.

"I'll stand back, but if she doesn't bite, she's fair game."

Not what I want to hear from the fucker, but more than I figured he would give me. I might be his best friend and his president, but when it came to women, he was a wild card at best.

"Here ya'go boys, two Bourbon Barrel Ales. Can I get you anything else?"

"Sit and talk for a bit Mama."

"Sorry I can't. Don't want to make a bad impression on my boss."

She starts to turn around but I grab her wrist and haul her ass down on my lap. She tightens her body and her nails dig into the arm I have currently wrapped around her waist, holding her down. I keep her from getting up, because I know if I let go she will run.

"Yo, Irish! Nicole's out of commission for a few."

"Got it Boss man." Nicole looks back at me then back toward Irish. She huffs and her blue eyes go large and wide, as understanding hits her.

"Do you always get what you want?"

"Usually," I answer honestly.

"So you own this place?" she asks, and her nails stop biting into my arm. Fuck me! Did it make me more appealing if she knows I have money too? That tastes like bitter shit right there.

"The club does."

She eyes me up and down. I hate that my having money impresses her, but the way she just wiggled her thick, perfect ass on my lap is driving me crazy. I could drive nails with my cock by this point.

She turns so she is straddling my lap, her hands come up around my neck and she pulls my face in closer. I grab hold of her hips and pull her down harder on me. Fuck yeah.

She moves her index finger along the side of my jaw line and down my neck. Her face moves closer to my ear and I can feel her hot breath.

"Mmm…Dragon, do you know what you're doing to me right now?" I feel her teeth bite into the side of my ear.

"Carrying you into the back and fucking you seven ways to Sunday?" I answer, my eyes mesmerized by her breasts, as she rotates her hips against my body.

She pulls up on my lap so one leg is on the floor and bends the other so her knee is along the top of my thigh. Fuck why did I ever think she was innocent? There's nothing innocent about the way….

"Giving me a damned good sexual harassment lawsuit you asshole!" she growls and then pushes her knee into my crotch. It wasn't as hard as it could have been, but damn it hurt.

She pulls away, grabs her tray and turns her back on me.

"Irish, I'm back on duty."

"Got it Nicole," he says, and I knew he was laughing, but I couldn't hear him over Crusher.

Crusher laughs so hard he has tears coming out of his eyes.

"Fuck that was fun to watch. I think I'm in love," Crusher says, as he watches the little witch sashay around the bar taking orders. She has obviously been a waitress before. She was damn good at it. Why a girl who drives a Mercedes is working as a waitress is beyond me. She is a puzzle and hell if that doesn't make her more interesting. There's also the fact that she resists my advances, when I usually have bitches begging for me.

I put the cold bottle of beer on my nuts, because damn it all to hell I needed to. I'm pissed off, but at the same time I am intrigued as hell. I like the battle. Nicole didn't know it, but she is waving a red flag in front of a bull and I'm going to fucking charge.

Nicole

It had been a week. One whole week of Dragon coming, in either flirting or just being broody as hell. Sad as it was, I am fast getting addicted to both. Sometimes he came in with men he called Crusher and Gunner, and sometimes with a huge ass bald man he calls Bull. Tonight it was Bull. He actually is my favorite. He rarely speaks, but it was a challenge to try and get him to. It had become a game for me. Tonight, I figure Bull will win, but that is only because I will be more distracted by Dragon than normal. This is hard to believe, even for me, but sadly true. I know this because I watch them come in and Dragon just looks so damned good tonight. He is wearing a sky blue t-shirt that stretches across his torso like a glove. He has on faded almost white, blue jeans and those brown eyes of his are even more intense. I don't bother to go ask for their order. I know the drill by now.

"Hey boys, you're running late tonight," I say, trying to avoid looking into Dragon's eyes. I set down two house brews and wink at Bull. As usual, he says nothing, but it seems like his eyes might have danced a little. Probably not, but I wanted to think so.

"Nicole."

I swallow almost afraid to look. Dragon and I have been doing this dance for a while now. I know it and he does too and soon enough it is going to happen. I am losing my strength. He makes my legs weak and I want a taste of whatever he keeps promising.

The only thing holding me back is I'm just a little afraid of him. He is a player and I am a novice with men. One thing I am totally and definitely sure of, is that Dragon will leave his mark on me. I'm just not sure how deep it will go and that unknown is why I am trying to fight it. I'm weakening though and I know Dragon senses that.

"Dragon," I say, hoping like hell I sound bored and not the bundle of nerves I actually am.

"We need to quit playing this game Mama."

"I agree. You should give up and go find a Twinkie," I say boldly, even though it kills me. Part of me wishes he would, because that would give me an excuse to say no, when I really want to say yes.

I walk off going over to another table, before I beg him not to do that. The table is full of some regulars who come in to drink and wind down after a hard day of working on a local farm. They are nice enough guys. They tip well and are fun to be around. One of them, Seth, has asked me out. He is good looking, in a young cowboy kind of way, with sunny blond hair and mischievous green eyes. Had I not been hung up on Dragon, I would have said yes a week ago. Trouble is, I am totally hung up on Dragon. It is taking all I have not to demand another kiss from him, or to give in to his numerous advances. Each time he finds a reason to put his hand on my back or my hip, each time he tucks a stray strand of hair behind my ear, each time he says my name in his gravelly voice...each time...each fucking time, I want to jump on him and ride him like a horse in the Kentucky Derby!

"Nicole, woman when are you going to feel sorry for a broken down ole' cow hand and go out with me?"

I laugh, I couldn't help it. I actually do like Seth. He just doesn't make my whole body come alive like Dragon did.

"Aw Seth, I don't think I could handle you babe," I say with my 'ole shucks' sass, which seems to up my tips.

It was either that or the way my breasts kept trying to bust out of my shirt. I was trying to be optimistic.

"Maybe not girl, but I'd make sure you'd enjoy trying," Seth replies easily as I gather up the empty bottles.

"You guys want another round?"

"Nah Sweetheart, stock sale is tomorrow, so I gotta get in early. Give me your pen," Seth answers.

I reach behind my ear where I keep my pen perched and hand it to him. He scribbles something down on a drink napkin and gives it to me, along with the pen.

"There. Call me. A bunch of us are planning on spending Saturday night out at Holly Bay under the stars."

I think he can see the 'no' coming because he holds his hand up in a 'stop' motion.

"Think it over, love to get to know you better babe, no pressure."

Yep, I would totally go out with him if not for the tall, dark, and broody man who I just know at this very moment is behind me. I know this because he reaches around and takes the napkin out of my hand and rips it up. The pieces fall on the table with a few drifting down to the floor. I concentrate on those pieces until they hit, trying to figure out how to handle this situation.

"The lady's not interested Baker. Look elsewhere," Dragon's voice rumbles in my ear, and the hot air sends chills down my back.

"Dragon, didn't realize you and Nicole were dating," Seth says, and he looks between me and Dragon. His eyes lock on mine and I see disapproval there. That kind of pisses me off, but I am busy trying to figure out how to tell Dragon to go to hell loud enough they might hear me about five states over.

"We're not." I turn to the side to look at Dragon. "What the hell are you doing?" I ask.

"Making sure men know my woman is *my* woman," Dragon says, with those big beefy arms of his crossed at his chest.

"When the hell did I become your woman?" I ask, while Bad Nicole is jumping for joy inside.

"The minute you gave me a taste of that mouth," Dragon answers.

"That was over two weeks ago and besides, what happened next made that kiss null and void," I argue, ignoring the heat that races up my face.

"What happened next? You mean when you wrapped your legs around me and tried to claw up my damned back?"

"No! I mean when you tried to get me to fuck your whole damn club!" I exclaim, before I realize what I am saying. Once it's out there though, there's not much I could do, besides die of humiliation.

The room goes quiet with the exception of the music playing in the background. I have always liked country music. Now though, the sound of some man whining about going redneck crazy? I hate it.

"Woman, you got legs?" Dragon asks. I look at him like he is insane, and it's a good possibility.

"Yes and I'm using them to walk away from you."

He grabs me before I can.

"You control who opens and closes your legs yeah? I ain't making or asking you to do shit."

"You insinuated!" I argue.

"You put words in my mouth Nicole, that's on you."

"You're so full of shit Dragon. We both know what you said."

"Maybe we see it differently. Ask Bull what I told him I'd do if he touched your ass."

I start wondering if I could kill him with laser beams of death shooting out of my eyes.

"I don't need to ask Bull, because...."

"Bull, what did I tell you man?"

"That you'd cut my dick off if I tried to get it near your woman?" Bull's big voice thundered out into the quiet room.

"Well that doesn't matter because...."

"Got to tell you Mama, you take Baker here up on his offer and I'll give him worse. You're mine. You feel me?"

I look at his dark eyes and feel this nervous anxiety flutter through me. His words excite and trouble me.

"Um...Dragon, you realize that's a little crazy after just one kiss?"

"You want my mouth again? For that matter, do you want more from me woman?"

"I...I'm not sure, I need to think about this," I say honestly. He has me freaked out, I can freely admit that.

Dragon takes off and motions for Bull to follow him. They walk out the door. Shit, what does that mean? I look towards Irish. He's watching me, but he doesn't say anything. I sigh and get back to work, ignoring the looks I keep getting. Seth and his crew left shortly after and I breathe a little easier.

Out of the corner of my eye, I see Dani come in. She is working the poles tonight on the late shift. Irish had only given me earlier hours. I didn't mind, the tips were decent and this way I was home early and I enjoy that.

"What's up with you girl?" Dani asks, coming over to me.

"One guess," I answer. Since she already knew about the dance Dragon and I have been doing, it won't be a huge leap for her.

She snorts. "Girl, go ahead, give in and take him for a test drive. You know you are going to anyway." She said shaking her head.

"He got mad and left, so who knows what is going to happen."

Dani laughed harder. "I know girl. I've seen the way that hunk of beef looks at you."

I sigh and bite my tongue to keep from asking for details. "Go shake your ass, I'm headed home."

"See you later woman," she replies, and walks back towards the dressing area for the dancers.

"Later!" I call out to her back, trying not to concentrate on the sad feeling I have had since Dragon left. I find myself praying Dani is right and Dragon will be back. Shit.

Dragon

I gave myself the rest of the night and today to calm down. I am pissed at a lot of shit really. Nicole, even though she is mostly right and at first I had thought of her as Twinkie material, that changed when her smart mouth stood up to me. Something happens to me when she talks back. It annoys me, but soothes me at the same time.

Life was shit right now, between Nicole and my men being on edge. I am about to blow.

Small things have been happening that lead me to believe we have a mole in our midst, and that shit was a bitter pill to swallow. Today a shipment of narcotics we were guarding had been raided in the town before ours. Cops had been tipped off. That shit didn't happen without a narc being involved.

You have to be able to trust your brothers with your life and if you can't, there's no point in having them around. In fact, doing so could get your ass sent up, which just brings to mind another reason why life is so fucked up right now. I got word from some men locked up with Dancer, that my brother had been fucked up more than once in the last month by some fucking guards. They thought torturing a patched member of the Savage Brothers just because they could was fun. Dancer hadn't told me shit, and that has to fucking stop.

I nurse my beer trying to get a handle on everything going through my brain. Nicole's going back and forth from table to table. She needs to make a move soon.

Crusher is talking and I reply here and there, but I can't tell you what the hell he is yammering about. I hope my mumbled 'yeahs' don't come back to bite me in the ass.

Finally my girl comes over. She looks nervous, confused and sexy as hell.

"I see Tanya already got your beers," she says watching me closely, those blue eyes of hers calling to me like nothing I had ever experienced before.

"Yeah."

"You aren't sitting in my section," she said, and I knew that shit.

"I know."

That was a direct hit, but when her face paled, I didn't get the satisfaction I thought I would.

"Oh. Well I need to get back to work. I just thought, well, if you wanted." She pushed a folded sheet of paper towards me, her face flushed red. Then she walks away. Crush shakes his head at me. I ignore him, pick the note up from Nicole and saw it had her phone number on it. Finally! Fuck, she is turning me into some kind of pussy. I don't even know why I did things this way. I only know it was important she give in to me.

I walk over to where she is talking to a regular. I can't even remember his name. Right now I can't remember anything other than this woman. I stand behind her and she stops talking and turns to me.

"Look Dragon, I don't..."

I didn't let her finish. I put her serving tray on what's-his-name's table, and then I bend down enough so that my shoulder pushes into her breasts, while my arm goes around the backs of her knees and I lift her up and over my shoulder.

"What the hell are you doing? Put me down Dragon! People are staring! You can't just..."

I reach up and slap her ass hard, not as hard as I eventually would, but hard enough she should have gotten the message. Her hands begin beating on my back and she tries to wiggle to get away from me. I guess she didn't.

I slap her ass again, harder this time.

"Ouch! Dragon! Damn it that hurts!" she says and her voice sounds shaky. I am hoping it isn't fear. I don't hurt women, but I do like control and she needed to learn this on her own. She would eventually.

"Then behave," I answer, rubbing her ass where I had swatted her, all the while walking to the back office. We make it there and I close the door, shutting out the laughter behind us. I slowly put her down so she stands in front of me. Her hands immediately go back to her ass.

"What on earth are you doing?" she asks, taking a couple of steps away from me.

"Teaching you a lesson."

"You have no right to teach me anything! We don't even know each other."

"You gave me that right weeks ago and you sealed it tonight by giving me your digits. Now get your pretty little ass over here before I tan it again."

"I'm keeping my ass as far away from you as I can. I should have gone with my first instinct! You're insane," she responds, taking a few more steps backwards.

"Wrong answer Nicole! Now stop walking away from me," I growl at her and she instantly freezes.

She doesn't know all the sides of me just yet. I might like fire in a woman and hell, with her I'm discovering I like it even more than I knew, but I also like obedience. She'll learn it. At just the mere thought of her bowing to my commands, my dick jerks. Poor thing is swollen so hard I will have permanent teeth marks from my zipper. Hell, it might be good if I make her kiss every damn one of them.

She finally stops backing away but only because she hit the wall.

"We have a few things to get straight Nicole."

"You're freaking nuts! I thought we'd get to know each other! Until recently, I didn't even know you existed."

"Now you do and baby, I know a lot about you."

"You don't," she argues looking around the room for another exit. Too bad, since I currently have the only one blocked. Sorry baby, you're not getting away this time.

"I know how you taste when you kiss. I know the feel of your moan in my mouth when I tease your tits. I know the feel of your fucking delicious ass when you're turned on, and I know the way you get wet when a man takes control of you."

I watch the blush roll over her face and it fucking makes me feel ten feet tall. I'm a dark man and things have touched me that would shrivel a weaker man's soul. Nicole was pure white in that world. A glimpse of something I never thought I would have, but I sure am not going to pass it up.

I had this beauty all pegged wrong. She's not Twinkie material. Hell, it wouldn't surprise me if she's totally innocent. Fuck me, what would it feel like to be the first inside that tight little pussy?

"Dragon, seriously you're freaking me out here. We don't

know each other."

"I've heard this song from you before, time for a new one," I say, walking towards her as if she was my prey, and right now she is.

"Had I known you were going to go all psycho on me, I wouldn't have given you my number!" she cries out and I can hear the panic in her voice.

I am not about to give in on this. When you've lived the life I have, you learn to go after what you want. I want her. I'm going to have her. I've decided there's only one way to get her out of my system, and I need to get her out of my system. It's a scary ass feeling when your dick doesn't cooperate with your need to get laid. So I'm going to give him what he wants, until he's ready to move the hell on.

"Fair enough. I'll ask you three questions and you answer honestly. If your answer is 'no' to any of the three, then I'll back the hell away and we won't ever have another conversation."

That seems to make her breathe easier. Silly girl! I let my smile go friendly, lean my arm beside her head against the wall and effectively block her in with my body.

"What are the questions?" she asks, like a spoiled little child who's not getting her way. Fucking cute!

"Did you think about me last night while you were in bed?"

A deep blush darkened on her cheeks. Fuckin' A she did.

"Only because you're a psycho!"

My smile deepens. We both know she's lying. I don't need to point that shit out.

"Did you think about me when you woke up this morning all warm and sleepy?"

She turns away and stares off to the side, refusing to look

into my eyes.

I put my hand up and used my thumb and index finger under her chin to pull her back around to me.

"Answer me Nicole."

She licks her lips. I look down at her breasts and her nipples are so fucking hard they look like diamond points sticking out under her shirt. Nice big fucking nipples too, at least the size of a dime. Oh hell, I can feel pre-cum gather on the head of my cock.

"It didn't mean anything."

"Okay, then one more question. Did your pussy get wet when I carried you in here and slapped that fucking fantastic ass of yours?"

She gasped. "No!" She looked at my face, but again her eyes avoided mine.

"I think you're lying, Nicole."

"I'm not," she argues. "So that means this game you're playing is over and I need to get back to work." She ducks under my arm, trying to escape. That's not going to work for me.

"Prove it."

She freezes instantly, her body taut. "What?" she asks, and her face is white now. Oh yeah baby, you played right into my hands.

"I said, prove it. If I didn't make you wet, then show me."

"How on earth would I do that?" she asks and I could almost see her heart beating out of her chest.

"Strip and show me your pussy. If you aren't dripping wet for me, if I can't see how wet your little pussy is for me, I'll leave you alone."

"I'm not going to strip for you! Are you insane, high, or both?"

I grin because really I hoped that would be her answer.

"So you're saying you're not going to strip for me?"

"That's exactly what I'm saying!"

"Well Nicole, I'm afraid you leave me with no other choice."

"Oh well Dragon."

I reach out and grab her arm and pull her into me.

"What...what are you doing now?"

"Well if you aren't going to show me sweetheart. I have to find out through other means."

"Other means?" Her voice comes out squeaky and it makes me smile.

"Yeah Mama," I say softly.

"What other means?"

I bend down to whisper in her ear, letting my breath fan her skin. "I'm going to slide my hand down in your pants, move my fingers over your pussy and see if you're telling me the truth."

"Dragon I think this joke has gone on long enough, I mean really I think its best...."

"Shhh baby," I say pushing her even flatter against the wall. I put her hands over her head and secure both of her small wrists in one of my hands.

I dart my tongue along the outer shell of her ear. I can tell by the way her body tightens, she likes it. She likes having her neck and ear played with. I file this information away. The way I look at it, this is a war and I need every weapon I can find at my disposal.

With that in mind, I whisper directly into her ear this time. "It's not like I'm going to fuck you baby. I just need to find out if you're lying to me. A good girl like you, you wouldn't lie would you Mama?"

I move my free hand down her neck. Her small collar bone is evident against her skin. I follow the long sexy line of her neck and shoulder and admire the way her ear is shaped. It begs to be sucked on and this might just become a favorite place to bury my face, except for her pussy and maybe her breasts. Shit how in the hell could a man choose?

I lightly tease the skin, moving down along her collar bone, lightly grazing one of her fucking perfect breasts, making sure to worry the nipple slightly with my thumb. Then I move along her rib cage and around to the front of her stomach. I leave my hand splayed across her abdomen, my index finger running gently back and forth over her belly button. My finger teases along the top of her shorts and I run my tongue along her ear again, before sucking on the lobe and nibbling it as I pull back.

"Would you Nicole?"

Her breath hitches and her hips thrust up against me, not much, but still the movement feels like I won the lottery.

I push my leg in between hers and rub it against her pussy with just enough pressure. At first she tries to get away, though I can tell it's a half-hearted attempt. Her eyes have taken on a glazed look. So fucking beautiful, I ache. I can't let her get her defenses back up, I need her more than I can ever remember needing anyone.

I've basically got her body trapped. Teasing her, I thrust my tongue into her mouth. I don't give her time to think, I force my way inside, leaving no part of her mouth undiscovered.

I let her know in that kiss I'm going to own her. I will. She needs to know there's no point in fighting it. Her tongue tangles with mine and the sweet taste of victory combined with her flavor makes me growl. She pushes against me now, but not to get away. Fuck no. Now, she's riding my leg like a champion.

"Nicole..." I say. My voice is hoarse but you can still hear the command in it. It's who I am. I need her to know that now, because I'm pretty sure with just this taste of her, we're both in trouble. It's going to be a long fucking time before I let her go. If I ever do!

"What..." she gasps as her eyes close.

I bend my head down and nip the hard nub poking through her shirt with my teeth, giving her just a sting of pain before I suck it into my mouth, shirt and all. She lets out a sound somewhere between a gasp and a moan. I release her with a pop that seems to echo in the silence, admiring the wet ring around her shirt.

"Pay attention baby, I asked if you had lied to me."

"About what?" she asks, rocking her hips slowly against my leg and by this time, I don't think she realizes what she is doing or saying, and that makes me fucking ecstatic.

"Are you wet?" I ask, releasing the button on her shorts.

"Yes, God yes," she moans when I move my hand down into her panties. I groan at the heat coming off of her. Her movements stop and she's squeezing my leg so fucking tight. Shit, if it had been my cock she would have snapped the damn thing in half.

I'm so hard by this time I could literally drive nails. I had heard that saying my whole life and until this moment, I had no idea what it truly felt like.

She whimpers when I push my leg against her pussy— harder this time. I'm rewarded with her small sigh of pleasure that contains my name. I pull her shirt over her head and toss it on the desk.

Nicole stands before me like a fucking goddess. Her dark blonde hair lies in waves, framing her face that is flushed with pleasure. Every now and then the light would catch the lighter blonde streaks and shine. She's breathing heavy and each breath she takes causes those large, perfectly shaped globes of her breasts to shake. The nipples are hard and somehow pebble even tighter when they hit the cold air of the room.

"Take the rest of your clothes off Nicole," I say quietly. I need this from her.

"Dragon, I…" She brings her hands up to try and shield her breasts from me. Goddamn it. I should have kept her my prisoner. Still, I need her to give this to me.

"Don't hide yourself from me Nicole. It's too late to go back. Take off the rest of your clothes."

"We…."

"Do it now, Mama." I keep my voice gentle, but the command is there too.

She swallows and rubs her lips together. I seriously thought she would back out. It would have hurt like hell, but I would have let her all the same. Instead, she surprises the hell out of me. She kicks off her shoes. Too bad, I think I might have liked her to leave those on. That thought is fleeting at best though, as Nicole reaches down and pulls her shorts off.

She's in nothing but a hot pink thong. The thin strip of silk barely covers her mound. She's gorgeous. No other word will fit. Her skin is a soft peach color that makes me want to taste every inch. Her breasts, fuck I know I keep thinking how big and juicy they are, but it's all my sex starved brain can think. I can't wait to explore them, feel them wrapped tight around my cock.

Her nipples, large and tight are begging for my touch. Her hips travel out in a curve that is feminine and sexy as hell, and makes me long to grab hold and take the ride of my life. I can't see her pussy but the part not hidden by the skimpy thong is bare. I can see the wet spot on the fabric though. It makes me hungry.

I take her hand and pull her toward Irish's desk. Sweeping my hand across it, I knock a bunch of shit to the floor with a loud clattering sound.

Nicole gasps and jumps as I startle her. I can't help it though. I need her and by God I'm going to take her.

"I've been thinking about this for weeks Mama," I growl pulling the thin strap of her thong with my hands and ripping that damned thing off her. I pick her up and sit her on the desk, quickly.

"Dragon... maybe we should..."

I don't let her finish. My mouth slams down on her to stop her words. I can't hear her tell me no. Fuck that shit. I push into her mouth with a hunger I have never felt. I rape her mouth. It's not pretty, but it's true. My tongue forces in, conquers, devours and takes. Still, even through the loud roar of blood thrumming in my ears, I notice she seems as hungry too. She's right there with me and this time when I break away, she's not denying me.

"You want this," I say staring at her.

Her eyes are so filled with desire the blue color seems to glow. She nods.

"The words Nicole, I need the words Mama."

"I want this. I want you."

"Bring your knees up against your chest baby. Open for me."

I expected her to balk at the order. The fact that she doesn't pleases the fuck out of me. She opens that pretty pussy for me. She has a small landing strip that is covered in blonde hair. I've seen a lot of pussy in my time. That's just fact. I don't think I have ever seen a more beautiful woman than Nicole. As I watch her already soaked pussy grow wetter before my very eyes, my brain screams out one word I never thought it would. Mine!

I quickly push my pants down to my knees and I grab my aching cock and zero in on the spot I'm now viewing as my personal heaven.

"Dragon, no!" she gasps.

"Yes Nicole. We've gone too far to turn back now," I say, trying to ram home and forget she's trying to stop this.

"Condom, you have to use a condom."

Holy fuck! I never bareback it, and here I am about to sink into this woman without even a thought of a condom. Worse, I'm not real happy about stopping to put one on now.

Fuck. I reach down and pull my jeans up enough to dig out my wallet. Finding the condom there I pull it out, stuffing everything else back in my pocket.

I make short work of the condom and don't give her time to say anything else before I slam into her. I close my eyes as I feel her walls ripple against me. I hold still inside of her, letting her get accustomed to taking me all in. I can tell it's been awhile for her. She's tight as hell. I take a deep breath and rest my head against hers waiting for the signal she's ready for me to go on.

"Oh my God," she whispers shakily, and a ghost of a smile flashes on my lips. I smile a lot around her. I'm not a man who smiles. Her words get me though, they are not what I expected, but then again with this girl, nothing ever is.

"You ready Mama?"

"After that, I'm not sure."

"I'll take care of you. Wrap your legs around me," I whisper, my hand going to cup her ass and pull her even tighter.

That small shift sinks me deeper inside when she locks her legs around me. I know this is just the first night of many with Nicole. I may not understand it, but whatever this is, it's different.

Her nails dig into my shoulders as we begin a rhythm. I smile against her skin as I inhale her scent. I like the idea of her marking me.

"Oh God, Dragon, don't stop."

Crazy woman, like that was even an option at this point.

When we're at this angle, my face is at the perfect spot to suck on one of those hard nipples that have been torturing me all night. I devour it like a starving man and then capture the nipple between my teeth, sucking it hard. I would have thought it impossible at this point, but I can feel Nicole getting wetter.

"You like it when my cock is buried inside that juicy little pussy of yours, don't you baby. You love taking my dick. Say it," I growl, slamming into her harder.

With each plunge her breasts jump and her nails grab hold so tight, I know if I could look at my back right now there would be blood.

"Oh God Dragon, I'm close. Please... I..."

"I'll give you what you need Mama, but say the words."

"I love taking your... dick," she calls out as I ride her harder.

My fingers slide into the valley between the cheeks of her ass, but she's so far gone I don't think she notices at this point. I'm barely hanging on by a thread, but I'm not going to shoot my load before she comes. That is NOT happening. I bite on her neck, getting a little rougher as she moans her approval. I growl, while tongue fucking her ear. She moans hotly and her nails slide down my back now, burning like hell the entire time. Does she mean to mark me? She definitely is and I'm not just thinking about her nails.

"Come for me Mama! Let it go, I'll catch you. Now Nicole," I whisper in her ear. I feel her body begin to convulse, her pussy clamping tight against my cock and milking me. I've never felt anything as good as what is happening right now with this woman. It's so fucking strong, she pulls me in with her to the abyss and my cry of release merges with her moans. It's a beautiful fucking song.

Nicole

Oh my God, I'm a whore! Those are the words that are playing in my head as I watch Dragon pull up his jeans. Yes, he is pulling up his jeans. He didn't even get undressed! Not like Super Whore Nicole! I'm currently curled up on a couch that Dragon carried me to after being fucked to an inch of my life. I'm pretty sure he short circuited what small brain cells I had and totally paralyzed me, and that's the only reason I can come up with for NOT covering my naked ass up. Shit what do I know? Super Whore Nicole may just be lying here waiting for round two with Fat Tommy outside! After all, whores do everyone right? Even FREAKING FAT TOMMY! Oh my God! I'm a whore!

"Get dressed woman before I fuck you again," Dragon orders. His voice, gravelly and dark sends chills up my back.

I swallow and then lean down to grab the clothes he had thrown on the floor. I don't speak. I'm not sure I can. The only words that come to mind are, Super Whore! *She's able to leap from man to man with a single...*

"Did you hear what I said?"

I'm pulling my shirt over my head when I look up at him. Fuck no I didn't hear him. Why can't he just leave?

Shit, I just had sex with a biker who has Twinkies for God sakes! I have to go get a damn shot. DO THEY EVEN GIVE CLAMYDIA SHOTS?? I mean he wore a condom, but can that shit eat through latex? He probably fucks so much he has a weird Teenage Mutant Ninja strain of it!

"Yo! Mama! I asked what time your shift is over."

Over? It'll never be over! Shit now my brain is quoting cheesy Nicholas Sparks movies.

I clear my throat. "Midnight, I get off at midnight."

God I hope we get off again.

Cue Bad Nicole, I'm so fucking screwed.

You can say that again.

I shake my head to clear the voices. I take some deep breaths. I feel better now that I'm not naked as a jaybird. I'll be fine. All I have to do is pull up that damned armor that I keep in place. It should be easy. I've used it since I was old enough to realize my parents had frozen popsicles for hearts.

I walk towards the door and Dragon stops me.

"I'll pick you up after work, babe," he says and kisses my forehead.

It's a sweet touch that sets butterflies off in my stomach. I ignore them and instead concentrate on being relieved. If he had really kissed me, I probably would have never come back out of it. He's that potent. He is Super Whore kryptonite even. I nod. If I disagree out loud he will fuck me into submission.

Yes please.

Bad Nicole needs to go—like yesterday! I clear my throat.

"I better get back to work."

"Okay Mama," he says, while his finger moves gently back and forth on my cheek. I open my eyes, and really I'm so far gone I don't remember closing them. I get lost in the dark chocolate of his eyes, so deep and intense. If he tried, he could probably see right through me.

He bends down further this time and lightly kisses my lips. It's sweet, totally unexpected after what we just shared. Then again, so was the forehead kiss. It seems totally out of character. I can't really say though because I DON'T KNOW HIM! Oh! My! God!

Then he's gone. The door closes and I'm left staring at the dumb thing, slightly in shock. I run my fingers through my hair because I'm sure at this point I look like I've just had sex on my bosses desk. BECAUSE I HAVE! I take a deep breath and close my eyes. Then I take another one... and another. Finally, I open my eyes and lick my suddenly dry lips. It's time I go back out there. I don't want to. I hate to face the world when they most assuredly know what I did in here. Shit.

Another fortifying breath, which didn't fortify at all, and I walk out with my head held high...okay, medium high. Whatever!

I grab my serving tray off the bar, having no idea how it got there at this point. I refuse to look my boss in the eye.

"Back on duty," I mumble.

"K, Nicole."

I can hear the laughter in his voice. I choose to ignore it. That's my plan, and I'm sticking to it.

I don't know where Dragon and his crony went. I'm trying not to dwell on it. I know he said he would be back to pick me up. Um. Yeah, I can't do that. I just need to get back home and pretend tonight didn't happen. Chances are Dragon left here and found another woman already. I ignore the pang of hurt that lodges in my stomach with the thought.

The crowd is starting to die down. There may be ten people in here. I'm collecting empties and wiping off Fat Tommy's table. I'm relieved to find that apparently my whoredom centers only on Dragon and not the sweet, but bald, beer belly, tobacco chewing Tommy who I learned ten minutes on the job—was a regular. All was not lost, I suppose.

I look up at the bar to find Irish watching me. He's been doing that a lot since I screwed Dragon in the back room. How could he not? Hell, he probably figures I'll spread my legs for him next. What was I thinking? I wasn't thinking, that much is clear. This whole night has one word attached to it. Mistake, a big mistake!

Dragon already wanted me to be a Twinkie and that had pissed me off! Then I go and act like one!

It's ten till ten and I am supposed to get off at ten. Yeah, I know I lied to Dragon. What's lying when I'm already a fornicator? Geez I'm losing it.

"Hey Irish, I'm going to cash in," I say not looking at him. Even avoiding his gaze, I can still feel the heat rise in my face.

"Thought Dragon was coming back to pick you up?" he asks, and I can feel fear spike through me and speed up my heart beat.

"Something must have come up. No worries, I have my own car. I'm sure he'll find me." I tried to sound breezy and carefree. I failed.

I paste on a fake smile and go over to the register to cash out. Luckily I had gotten good at this over the years and my money and orders jived. The only bad spot I have is when Irish mentions he should give Dragon a call. I ignore him. A customer demanded his attention and thankfully a crisis is diverted.

I am just about to leave when I feel a large hand cup my ass and squeeze it. For a minute I thought Dragon had shown up early and I'm not sure if it was fear or happiness that flitted through me. I knew after just a second though, that it wasn't Dragon's hand on me. The touch felt…wrong. I hate that I explain it that way, but it's true nonetheless.

"Irish, you didn't tell me you were getting some new talent."

My spine stiffens and I straighten up, trying to will myself into the wood of the bar to get some space between me and the voice behind me. He's got a deep voice, almost sexy, but something about it sends a warning through me and raises the hairs at the back of my neck, and not in a good way. I could tell he sat down on the stool behind me. This was bad news since every stool around me is empty. I lower my head at the bad luck I seem to be having. Apparently, I broke a mirror and somehow forgot.

"Hands off, Skull."

"Shit no, haven't seen a piece this fine in months. What's your name, chica?" he asks my back. I didn't want to turn around. That doesn't seem to matter; he wraps his arms around my stomach and pulls me onto his lap.

I take a breath and put my hands on his to pry them away from my stomach.

"Let me up Stud, I think you have me confused here," I said, trying to joke my way out of this.

"No way, *Mamacita*. You and me are going to get better acquainted."

Okay, well bright side, I now knew unequivocally that I was not a slut. Why? Because Skull or whoever was a damn fine good looking man, but he was still creeping me out. His dark hair was shaggy, in a way you just knew he didn't try but still looked like a runway model for Calvin Klein. His eyes were brown not dark like Dragon's, but shiny and sparkly. He had an indention on his jaw that was sexy and a slight scar above his right eyebrow. He was a walking dream man and he was doing nothing for me, except annoying me.

When he started laughing and a few others joined in I looked around. Shit, was this place full of bikers? Skull had brought three other men in with him. Was this more of Dragon's crew? Hell I needed to get out of here, maybe even move back home at this point.

"Let her up, Skull. She's Dragon's property," Irish said. His voice had moved from easygoing to so still and dark it sent chills. Then his words hit me.

Dragon's property?!

Irish's words seem to make Skull's arms wrap tighter around me, so tight that for a minute it hurts. I'm getting upset by this point, for a number of reasons. First and foremost though, I want out of this man's arms. I want out of this bar before Dragon decides to come back and most importantly I want to be locked up nice and tight at home, away from the crazies that apparently were thicker than molasses in this damned town.

"I don't see a damned stamp on her," Skull growls and he yanks my hair hard to look at the back of my neck.

I wince at the pain. I can feel the sting and breathe in to stop the water from gathering in my eyes. That's it. I've had enough. Who did this ass think he was?

I relax my body to catch him off guard. When his arm loosens against me enough to allow it, I move to the side with a flirty smile. I can see the disapproval on Irish's face as he catches my ass wiggling on Skull's lap. Skull's hard and obviously packing but the feel of him leaves me disgusted. I don't let that show though, playing the part as I slide down his lap and turn so I can move my hand down his chest. I'm good at playing the dumb blonde. It's come in handy over the years. Hell it worked with Dragon before I became a whore! When I catch Skull's grin and the way he is sizing up my breasts, I almost roll my eyes. Seriously men are just too predictable.

"What's your name, little girl?"

"Nicole." I'm trying to make my voice sound breathless. That's not hard to do, since I'm pretty much panicking. I've got to get out of this damned bar before Dragon makes it back in.

"Nicole, huh? I like that, sweet one. How about we get better acquainted?"

Ugh, seriously?

"What do you have in mind?" I ask, slowly moving my hand down his chest. Another couple of inches and I'm going to twist his balls so tight maybe one of them will pop and the blood can go back to his brain, which is obviously deprived.

"Nicole, get your fucking hands off him."

Oh fuck. My hand immediately stops. Damn it all to hell. I go to get up and I can't step away because Neanderthal man has gone back to holding me tight. I release an aggravated breath and then because at least I now have moving room, whereas I didn't before, I bring my elbow hard back into his solar plexus. He immediately lets go and I get up.

"What the fuck?"

"That's for pulling my damn hair and grabbing my ass!"

"Nicole, get over here now," Dragon ordered. He didn't yell, but his voice was cold and deadly. A smarter woman would have obeyed. I have never been particularly smart though, especially when it comes to men.

"Will you quit ordering me around like some damned lap dog?" I huff. I turn to the bar and untie the small pocket like apron I have around my waist.

"Get your damned ass over here before I smack it."

Did he really just say that?

I'm not sure why it surprises me at this point, but it does.

"Seems to me Dragon, *la amiga* doesn't want shit to do with you."

"Fuck off, Skull. What the hell you doin' in my club uninvited anyway, motherfucker?"

"Right now, enjoying the scenery," Skull replies.

"She's hands off," Dragon growls, and I really need to stop liking the way he growls damn it!

"Didn't see your mark on her and she seemed to warm up to me pretty damn quick, *compadre*. I'm thinking I'm about to get my hands all over her."

Skull's men start laughing, and as annoying as that was, Dragon manages to top it.

"She belongs to the club."

Now I have been pretty calm all things considered. I mean if you set aside the mild freak out I had after boinking the hot ass scary biker dude, I have been calm. I was even ignoring being talked about like I wasn't in the room. But having it announced that I was the club's property? After I had already set his ass straight on that shit? Oh hell no.

"She can talk for herself," I say finally. I am feeling a hundred different things, and wasn't too sure how to deal with it all. So instead of trying to sift through it, I decide to grab hold of the one thing that fucked with my head the most.

"Nicole," Dragon said, and even I could hear the warning in

his voice. Any other time I might have listened, but not now.

I look down at Skull.

"What the fuck is this mark thing you keep talking about?"

Skull smiles, and he might be good looking, but that smile is scary shit. This man is dark, cold and scary.

"Dragon here likes to mark his personal bitches. He puts the club symbol on their neck. You girl, don't have that mark, so I figure you're fair game. I'm not much for loose pussy, but for you? I'll make an exception. I don't even care if you are club pussy."

"Why would you think I was *club pussy*?" I ask. Oh but I knew. I knew and the knowledge was twisting sour in my gut. I was an idiot.

"Dragon just said you belonged to the club." The emphasis was on club. Not Dragon, but the club. Skull knew my reaction and the way his grin spread made me physically ill. He knew what he was doing. He knew that would cut, he knew he was twisting the knife. It wasn't so much to get at me. It was more to upset Dragon. I understood that, but it didn't change things.

"Nicole get your ass over here now," Dragon orders. I saw the guy who was with him earlier go around and stand in front of Skull. I walked the opposite way, going towards the door, while giving Dragon a wide berth.

"Nicole."

"Fuck you, Dragon. I told you before I'm not ever going to be a club chew toy."

I stopped in front of the door when a thought occurred to me.

"Was that what we did in there? Were you trying me out to see if I would live up to the stable you already have?" I yell out.

Had I been of my right mind, I would have been mortified. I

would have noticed how horribly quiet the room went, and the way we had become the center of attention. Thankfully, that didn't hit me—at least not right then. I was more mortified that possibly the single best sexual moment I would ever encounter in my life had really been just a try out for being community pussy!

"Woman, stop your yammering."

"My yammering… What the hell does that even mean? I can't believe you! You asshole! I gave myself to you. I gave you the green light. I didn't give myself to your buddies. I don't want your buddies. I wasn't thinking about anyone's hands on me but you, and the whole time you were planning on me just giving out to anyone in your fucking club? If you want to give me away, then fuck you. Go back to your Twinkies."

"Woman, we had an hour in a freaking back room, not a honeymoon. Now get your fucking ass over here."

If he had slapped me it couldn't have hurt more. What was worse was he was right. He was totally right. I was acting illogical and completely irrational. It was two strangers hooking up in a back room of a seedy bar. It hurt but it was the truth, and Dragon was absolutely right. I didn't tell him that however. I'd cry on Dani's shoulder later. I decided instead to score a point the best I could and be done.

"I think you're overestimating it there, stud. You didn't last fifteen minutes, let alone an hour."

I delivered my verbal barb, feeling a little bit better when Skull's laughter rang out loud. I could even hear Dragon's own man laughing to my left.

Dragon said nothing, but I could feel the anger vibrating from him. Still, in for a penny, in for a pound and all that.

"I'm out of here Irish. I'll see you Friday."

"Yeah, alright. Friday," Irish said, laughing enough it distorted his words. I could see a muscle jump in Dragon's jaw.

I turned to go and stopped at the door when Dragon called out again.

"You walk out that door woman and we got problems."

I didn't turn around.

"It was a fifteen minute hook up in the back of a bar, Dragon. We don't have anything."

I thought it was a good parting line. Aces really, so I pushed the door open and left this horrible night behind.

Dragon

I watched her leave and wanted to go spank her ass. Women didn't talk back to me like that. Hell none had even tried. Nicole was going to be a spitfire to try and tame. I feel a certain amount of exhilaration at the thought. Still, I couldn't show weakness in front of Skull or his men. If he thought Nicole was special, he'd sail down on that shit like a fucking vulture.

So I shrugged when she left and relaxed the tension in my body. I'd be dealing with Nicole soon enough. I didn't exactly know how, but I would. I walk over to Skull's table and stop.

"I asked what the fuck you are doing on my turf unannounced, Skull. You and me, we got an agreement. You and the Devil's Fire stay out of our way and we'll stay out of yours. You going to start going back on that shit, maybe I need to rethink letting you use my town to get from Red River to run your shit."

"Just stopping by for a drink. Surely old friends can do that, eh?"

Smarmy motherfucker! We're not friends. He'd fuckin' slit my throat if he got the chance and I wasn't too far behind that my own damn self, especially after seeing his hands on Nicole. Skull was a waste of air.

"Deal was, you stay off Savage property and we let you use our road. That was the extent of the deal. No fuckin' thing else exists between us asshole."

I have to admit, I enjoyed the flash of hate that came over Skull's face. At least the feeling was real. I could deal with real. Not this fake shit he was trying to blow up my ass. I ain't got time for that.

"There's a nasty rumor going around, Dragon."

I yank a seat out and sit down. It looks like this shit was going to take a while. Nicole would get away with her shit for now.

"Not in fuckin' junior high, Skull. Don't have any idea about fucking rumors."

"Fine, I'll lay it out for you."

"Finally!"

Skull's jaw clamps down and I can almost hear his teeth grinding.

"Word has it you're letting the Kings traffic their merchandise in this area, for a cut."

"Word would be wrong."

"Have it on good authority, your man Twist was brokering *el trato* with them just last week. That does not work for me Dragon. I have been paying your fees. You going behind my back man, we have *problemas*."

"Are we havin' this discussion?" I growl, because now I'm pissed. For several reasons, but the majority of them have to do with the man in front of me.

He looks straight at me and doesn't back down, which isn't good. That means this fucker truly believes what he is saying.

"Don't have a deal with the Kings, haven't even talked to the motherfuckers. You had my word on this before. That's not good enough, perhaps you and I do have problems. Don't appreciate the disrespect."

Skull nods. I feel Crusher moving closer to my back.

"I got no problem with you man as long as our deal is straight up. I hear things, though."

"What things?"

"Not packing tales, Dragon. Like you said, it is not junior high. You just might want to reel in your boys though. That's all I got to say."

"I handle my men. You hear shit otherwise, then you be a man and speak up—or shut the hell up and get out of my club."

Skull slams his hand down and rakes a bottle onto the floor. I hear it break but I keep my face cold as stone. He didn't intimidate me; I have faced fuckers harder than him for years. Still, I couldn't back down from this, even if there was a chance Skull was telling the truth. You can't show any weak spots to an enemy. In this world that's the quickest way to die.

"Your ass man, I was trying to do you a solid. It will not happen again. Don't worry about if I am a man, *hermano*. I'll make sure your new *el gatito* knows this upclose and personal."

He got up and slapped me goodbye on my shoulder. I want to rip his arms off for even thinking about Nicole and for touching me. I didn't though. I remain expressionless and choke the need for violence down. No weaknesses! That was my world.

Crusher waited until Skull and his crew had left then took a seat. Didn't take a minute and Irish was in the other seat. They knew as well as I did, Skull had to know something or he never would have come into my territory.

"Should we talk to Twist? Find out what the fuck is going on?" Crush asked.

"Not wise." Irish spoke up and I agreed, but remained quiet.

"Why the fuck not," Crush asked. He had a history with

betrayal and I knew this shit would hit way too close to home for him.

"Because if this shit is true, we are just letting him know he's been found out. No, we have to figure this shit out first," I explained.

"He's a brother. Shouldn't we go to him directly? We owe him more than taking a fuck face like Skull's word over one of our own."

I agree with Crush to a point, but the truth was I knew Skull well enough to know he wouldn't put the word out unless he could back it up. I had known Twist for a while, but I couldn't lie. There was a lot about the man I didn't like. There was a reason I had never promoted him into a higher position in the club. He joined up about the same time as Bull. They had served a term in the military together. Bull came across as a straight shooter, but Twist? Well he lived up to his name at times. Twisted shit up a hundred ways before it finally fell into place. If Skull said he had heard talk, then yeah, he had more than heard it.

"Get Bull, Hawk and Gunner together, have them meet up with us at the shed tomorrow. Keep it quiet. We'll have a vote."

Crush nodded. Irish was Irish. He didn't say shit, but he was with me.

I had hoped that would be the end of it and I'd get out of here. I should have known better.

"So?"

"Shut it Irish."

"I'm just saying she seems like a firecracker. Maybe more trouble than she's worth."

Undoubtedly, the word popped to mind at the same time my

dick jerked at the thought of her again.

"Hell I like a woman with spirit. If Dragon ain't up to it, I'll take her off his hands in a heartbeat."

"You want to keep your hands then you keep them the fuck away from her," I order.

Nicole might have thought I wanted to share her. Hell, I can't even deny I hadn't thought about it initially. I had done that before with some of my brothers, and it never bothered me. Yet when I had seen Nicole's hands on Skull and that son of a bitch looking at her tits, I could have easily choked the life out of the asshole. Yeah there would be no sharing Nicole, at least not until I worked the bitch out of my system.

"Whoa you're sounding awful territorial there brother," Crush said, watching me closely. Crush and I had a long history. It went deep. He knew me inside and out. He could tell this was different. I didn't want to talk about that shit though. This wasn't some kind of Steel Magnolia's moment when we would start acting like a bunch of pansy assed bitches, gushing about feelings. I wanted Nicole. That's all I needed to concentrate on right now.

"Fuck off," I return only half joking. "I'm out boys. See you tomorrow. Crush you and me will leave early to get to the shed."

I didn't look back. I didn't wait for them to reply. I had one thing on my mind and I know they knew what it was, and I didn't need to see their smart assed faces mocking me.

Dragon

I didn't go to see Nicole like I wanted. I thought about it. Fuck I hadn't thought about much anything else since I had sunk inside her. Still, she needed to stew over shit for a bit. I wanted her, but I'll be damned if I'm not going to demand respect from her sexy tight little ass.

It had been over twenty four hours now since I had been inside the damned woman and I had never been a junkie, but I felt like if I didn't get my fix soon I would start shaking with the need. Fuck. That woman has me so damned knotted up inside, I'm starting wonder if she didn't put some kind of voodoo hex on my cock.

I need to get my head in the game quick, like yesterday. I'm currently sitting in front of a worn out as hell table made from an old slab of wood. My chair cocked back, my feet perched on the table, giving the appearance I am a man without a care in the world. Hell I couldn't even remember what being a man like that felt like. Truthfully, I don't think I had ever felt like that—not that it fucking mattered. Life was what you were dealt and mine had been shitty since the beginning, but I survived and fucking did it daily.

I had called a meeting at the shed and Bull and Gunner had just arrived. Hawk, Irish and Crush had all come with me.

This place was well off the beaten path. It was an old fishing cabin in the hills out from Laurel Lake. You had to drive up a road with so many curves and turns it felt like you would kiss your own ass before it was done. Once you got all the way back on the hill, the brothers and I had hidden some ATV's in a small garage that was out of sight, right off the main road. It was visible, but hidden enough you would have to look for it and know it was there to even see it. It was a building we had dug out of the side of a hill. The place was in fact, part of the hill itself and we encouraged the kudzu vines and other shit to grow wild all over the place to hide the damn thing.

Once you got on the ATV and traveled about thirty minutes, you arrived at the shed. It had 3 rooms and a completely different building about thirty feet away. The brothers and I fixed the place up when we first formed the club. We needed a place out of sight, so we could make sure we kept people in line. It wasn't easy being the ruling club of a city. There was always someone wanting to take that position away from us. The shed and the reason we used it, weren't my favorite parts of the life, it was just a fact. It was a dog eats dog kind of world and you had to do what you had to do.

"I still say it's fucking cold to test a brother. He's been part of our damned group for years now. He should have our respect," Crush said, drawing my attention back to the conversation at hand.

I understood his point but I was getting damn tired of being questioned. It was my fucking club. My word was law. It had to be and it wasn't that I was a hard ass with a god complex. Screw that shit. No, it was that my decisions kept our asses alive and I needed them to have my back—not question me. Crush was a good man, and one of my closest brothers but I was fucking tired of this shit.

"Enough. I fucking heard you the first fifteen damned times you spouted that shit. I'm not fucking asking for your permission dick weed, I'm informing you of my fucking decision. Respect that shit or get the fuck out."

"I'm just saying…"

"I know what the fuck you're saying, but this is not the first fucking time Twist has been called out. Shit, it's not even the second. I'm sick of fucking dealing with this. I can either trust a brother or I can't. Skull can be an asshole, but he shoots straight. If he says he's heard talk and mentions a name, then that means the motherfucker has seen that shit up close and personal."

I look at my brothers, and they were my brothers, and I knew I was a fucked up looking S-O-B. I was big and broad. I worked hard for that. You couldn't really be the president of an MC and look like a damn science nerd. My dark skin was marred with scars and tats and my hands were callused and rough as shit. I didn't care. It was who I was.

My brothers though? Each one was different. Crush had dark hair and skin tanned naturally by the sun. He liked the military and kept his buzz cut going, though maybe a little longer than regulation since he got out. Irish had strawberry blond hair, which was shaggy and cut with no real direction. I secretly thought he just took the scissors and chopped off a whack of hair when it annoyed him. His skin was so fucking white! Damn shit made me want to put on my shades when he went around without a shirt. Bull? He was a brother, like me. There wasn't much pretty about him that was for damn sure, even though it took him a freaking hour to shave his head bald. You would think he was a pretty boy, but wasn't. He was quiet and rarely smiled. As club enforcer that shit worked though. Gunner and Freak were different as night and day and they were real brothers. Freak was covered in tats, hair that was thick and long and covered most of his face because he didn't give a shit. Gunner was blonde, blue-eyed and could have been a surfer dude. He didn't really fit in with our rough ass crew. I liked him though. He was a straight shooter and I figured he'd be the one to have trouble with this shit, since he brought Twist in. He was remaining quiet though. I appreciated it. Now if Crush would quit dogging my ass about it. I had shit I wanted to do tonight. Namely Nicole, damn bitch had me dying for her again. She was going to be deep trouble. I knew it. Fuck, I saw it coming head on, but I couldn't stop that shit. I didn't even want to.

"Are we done with this fucking convo now boys, or do I have to sit here and watch you jerk your dicks before I can leave?" I growl. Crush gave me a pissed off look but he nodded with the others.

"Then it's settled. Gun, Twist trusts you. You hang by his side both when he knows and especially when he doesn't. Freak you are there when Gun ain't. You get so far in his shit, you gotta shower."

"We hear ya Boss," Freak said. Gunner just nodded his silent agreement. That was his way. Man didn't talk much. It might weird some out. Me? Hell no. I knew when Gun talked I should listen, so it worked.

"Crush, you and Bull get started on your roles in this shit fest. I need answers by yesterday. I need to know what's going on this week, before we find ourselves in a fucking mess."

"What if the man is innocent and we do this shit to him? What then Drag?" Crush questioned me yet-a-fucking-again. At least this time he didn't sound like a damned sullen little bitch face about it.

"Then I take him to the fucking side and man up. But, this fucking shit? It's our life. Club comes first and ain't no motherfucker above suspicion when the safety of our lives and our fucking livelihood is on the line. You feeling me here Crush?"

"Yeah man I got ya."

"Then church is mother-fucking-adjourned. Smoke' em if you got' em but I'm off. Got somewhere I need to fucking be and it ain't with you pricks."

"Hold up Boss, I'll head out with you." I was already heading for the door but it didn't surprise me to hear Gunner. He had been silent, but he brought Twist in, so he'd want to give me shit about this I'm sure. I appreciated him holding that shit in though in front of the others. If he and Crush both questioned my decisions, this meeting would have been a lot worse and definitely bloodier. They may be my club brothers, but as the president, if I needed to knock heads together to prove there was a reason I was their leader, then I would.

We were halfway back to our bikes when Gunner finally spoke up, but what he said wasn't exactly what I was expecting.

"Hey boss, I'm sorry. If this shit is true, then it's on me and I didn't mean to put the club in danger."

"If this shit is true, it's on Twist not you Gun."

"I brought him in. Gave him my vote to get him on prospect status and petitioned for him to be added to the inner team. That's on me," Gun said, and you could hear the regret in his voice.

"If this shit holds and we find out Skull isn't blowing smoke up our asses, then Twist made those decisions on his fucking own. You can't take the responsibility for that shit. You always put your brothers' first Gun. I know that. The brothers know that. Rest easy man and don't get your tits all knotted up about that shit."

I knew what Gun was feeling, I had been in his position and it sucked.

He gave a weak smile I saw out of the corner of my eye. We pulled the side by side ATV into the garage area and bailed out.

"Want to head out to Pussy's for a drink?"

Pussy Willow was a club operated strip joint where the men liked to hang out—for obvious reasons. Any other night I would have said yes. Before Nicole I would have said yes to a hell of a lot more than a drink. Since I had tasted that sassy woman, it wasn't going to happen. There's only one woman and one pastime on my mind. It's not any of the bitches at Pussy's, and it's not drinking.

"Nah man, I got plans."

"Crush mentioned some chick. We going to be seeing her at the club soon?" He asks as we reach our bikes.

"I'm thinking affirmative on that brother," I said straddling my ride.

"Good stuff. Club needs fresh blood."

"No brother. This one is off fucking limits," Gunner was a damn good looking man, all Californian, easy going, blonde hair and blue eyes. Fuck no he wasn't getting around my woman.

When I realized what I was thinking, my fucking hands shook.

Chapter 2

Nicole

I never claimed to be the sharpest tool in the shed. I had spent the last day and a half berating myself for everything I had allowed to happen with Dragon. Different thoughts ran through my mind. I could tuck tail and run back to Blade. I could quit and find a different job. I could pretend whatever happened between me and Dragon (and yes, I was leaning towards this one) never happened.

Except it did, we got laid and fucked and we want it again.

Bad Nicole was a mean spiteful bitch and a whore, and her voice in my head was annoying. What Bad Nicole wasn't, well she wasn't wrong. I have never felt like that before. Dragon touched and awakened spots in me I never even knew existed. A girl could get addicted to the feelings he brought out in her.

So instead of sleeping at 11:58 p.m. on a Tuesday night, I'm sitting on the couch watching an October Scream and Scare Marathon on TV. I'm currently on Halloween ....who the hell knows what version or number? I'm curled up on the couch in my fuzzy red pajama pants with hot pink hearts all over them, a white baby doll t-shirt and big pink fuzzy socks. My hair is pulled up on top of my head in a ponytail-bun-gone-wrong combination, and I just polished off a pint of chunky monkey ice cream. I might be in the midst of a depression. Dani is out with some boy toy and the house is too damn quiet. So ice cream seemed like the only solution. I miss Dragon.

There I said it. I kind of expected him to stop me from leaving the bar. I was disappointed when he didn't. I was okay though, totally fine. Then, time kept passing and I haven't heard a word from him. Seems that should clue me in. I am definitely the whore I originally pegged myself as, and Dragon got what he wanted. He's probably sunk deep inside some cupcake now.

I refuse to call them Twinkies. I happen to like Twinkies and knowing Dragon called his whores that would ruin Twinkies for me. Of course as I think this, I am studiously avoiding the view of my kitchen table. I might have accidentally poured out the contents of a Twinkie box, and I might have accidentally flattened them with the bottom of my umm..third or fourth glass of raspberry vodka and sprite. I could probably use another glass, but the cream that's all over the glass from the exploded plastic wrapped goodies annoys me. So, I don't. Instead, I lie here watching some bubble-headed ho bag get chopped up on the TV screen. Seriously, does it always have to be the blondes and why on earth are they always half dressed?

I pull the warm throw down off the back of the couch and snuggle up. When Dani and I first got here the weather was sunny and warm and in the high seventies. Now, it's dreary, rainy, and cold and I think the TV said it was like forty-two degrees outside. I figure that is somehow Dragon's fault too, I just don't know how to blame him yet. I should go to bed and sleep, but I tend to think more of Dragon there, so I refuse to.

I must have dozed off. I'm not sure for how long, but Michael Myers has been replaced by a killer dog, so lovely. I blink my eyes a few times trying to focus, when the banging on the front door begins. That must have been what woke me.

I get up stretching and yawning, thinking that if Dani is

going to try and beat me for slut of the week, the least the bitch could do was remember her keys.

I cup my hand over my mouth yawning so big, tears leak from the sides of my eyes.

I unlatch the door and freeze. Dani isn't there. No, staring at me through the screen security door is Dragon in all his glory. He looks good tonight. A woman couldn't deny that. He's wearing a Kelly Green t-shirt that's stretched over his biceps and his wide chest. It pops against his dark skin and I wish I could tear the shirt off and see more of what is underneath. I stare at him, not sure what to say and immediately get sucked into his dark chocolate eyes.

"What the fuck?" He barks.

Well hello to you too.

I think it, but I don't open my mouth. Maybe I short-circuited. I truly don't know what to say to him. He could be every woman's dream until he opens his mouth.

"What the fuck Nicole?" he barks again. If his voice wasn't so deep and raspy it would be annoying as hell about now.

I yawn again and I'm too brain dead to remember to cover my mouth this time, so I guess Dragon can see down to my tonsils. I shake my head trying to clear the sleep from it.

"What time is it?" There, a complete sentence, I'm getting better.

Give the girl a cookie. Shut up bad Nicole.

"Do I look like a fucking Timex? Open the door." Dragon…well yeah he barks yet again.

"You come to my house at this time of night, so I figure you at least know the time. I'm too tired for this. I'm going back to bed, adios Dragon."

"Unlock this damn screen door Nicole, I'm tired."

I stop the main door from closing and study him for a minute. There are times to fight and times to let it lie. I'm thinking right now, I should go for the latter. I missed him. I had sex with him. He was here.

I unlatch the door and turn around, heading back into the living room and my comfy bed on the couch. I plop down on the couch pulling the afghan up around me, bringing my knees up against my chest and wait. I hear the door close and the sound of the lock turning. It should make me nervous but it doesn't. I should question everything I do around Dragon but I don't. This is not normal.

"We shouldn't have had sex," I blurt out, watching as he walks to me. He stops in front of me and crosses his arms. I bite my lip wondering what will happen next. I don't think I can have sex with him again. I want to, God do I want to. Still, I need to jump back into reality, where you didn't just jump into bed with a man you didn't know. That led to madness and venereal diseases. Oh God, I needed to make an appointment at the free clinic tomorrow.

"What the fuck are you doing opening the door this late at night?" Dragon asked, still looking at me.

Okay... well alright... not what I expected.

"I thought you were Dani," I said trying to avoid looking at him directly. Whenever I did it seemed my brain short circuited.

"You don't open a door without knowing who the hell is out there Nicole."

"How do you know my name is Nicole?" Ignoring him and changing the subject.

"You're just now asking this? After what has gone down

between us and the back and forth dance we've been doing?" he asks. He is looking at me like I am crazy—which maybe I am, at least when I am around him. Then, he takes a deep breath and sits down beside me, turning so we are facing each other.

I shrug.

"Your girl used your name," he says, evidently giving up on my safety lesson.

"No she didn't. She called me Nic. You just assumed it was Nicole," I argued.

He took another weary breath. I didn't think it was because he was having trouble breathing. I pretty much understood it was to show I was being an idiot. I guess I was. I didn't really care though.

"What else would your name have been?"

"Nikita, Nikki, Nickel, Nicorette…." I ramble.

"Nicorette, like the fucking smoking gum?" he asked incredulously.

"Technically I think it's to stop you from smoking."

"Are we really having this discussion right now Mama? I'm beat."

"Umm… then why are you here?"

"Why wouldn't I be?" he counters and damn that is kind of a good question.

"We can't have sex again."

He nods his head, "Oh yeah we can mama."

"We can't. We don't know each other. I know what you think I am Dragon, but seriously, I'm not. I don't do things like we did. So, we can't do it again."

"What are you?" he asked quietly sounding tired.

"A woman who casually has sex, a good time girl!"

"Jesus, a good time girl?" He shakes his head, "Mama you might be the strangest woman I have ever met."

"Probably," I mumble.

"You've had sex before," Dragon says, as his hand moves up to my face to push some of my bangs away from my eyes.

His touch feels nice. I like the way his callused fingers tickle the skin under my eye. Was it my imagination or did he seem disappointed I've had sex before?

"Of course, but I knew them really well. I'd even dated them for a while. I know nothing about you. We've yet to go out on a first date!"

Dragon's fingers had been caressing my neck, but by the time I had stopped talking, his fingers had stopped moving. Damn it.

"I don't date Nicole."

"You don't what?" I ask dumbfounded.

"I don't date."

"Dragon, everyone dates."

"I don't."

I don't really know how to respond. It seems unreal, but I can tell he is completely serious.

"Like ever?"

"That's what I said, Mama."

"How can you tell if you like a girl if you don't even know her?" I ask and something about this conversation hurts me.

"I fuck her."

Oh. My. God!

"You... I don't even know what to say to that."

Dragon seems to get agitated. His face went from being somewhat soft (though I'm not sure it could ever go completely soft, he was too harsh), to being tight. There is also a vein popping along the side of his neck.

"Nothing to say, Mama it's just the truth."

"That's unreal."

"I'm not shiny and new Nicole. I've fucking been around the block. I've got scratches and dents and a lot of fucking miles. I'm a classic and not just anyone can handle me. I'm not about to make apologies for that shit. I am what I am."

"A classic?"

"Only ride worth a damn is one that's been around awhile and knows the curves in the road."

"Been around awhile? I can see that. That must be why there's so much rust. God I can't believe you. You're such an ass."

"Whatever woman, I'm tired. Let's get in bed."

"Um, this is my house," I said.

Dragon stands up and without even asking, yanks my afghan away.

"Hey stop that! I'm cold!" I complain reaching for it, but he threw it on the chair across from us before I could.

"That's why we're going to bed, so I can warm you up."

"Dragon you can't sleep here."

"Nicole, I can," he counters and bends down and picks me up like I weigh nothing. It was a strange feeling and if I hadn't been panicking over Dragon informing me we would be sleeping together tonight, I might have enjoyed it.

"We shouldn't. We should get to know each other better first."

"I was planning on just sleeping tonight Mama, but I told you how I get to know women. If that's what you want, I can change my plans. It'll have to be quick though, because I'm beat girl."

"Uh… we could just sleep."

It was then that I knew I was in trouble—like really big trouble. Because it was then that I saw a complete miracle. Dragon smiled. Holy hell! He was a walking wet dream before, but a smile? A real one, the kind that lit up those dark eyes of his and caused angels to weep. Christ.

Dragon carried me upstairs and I directed him to my room. Once there, he slowly let me slide down his body until I stood in front of him. He moved his hand around to undo my hair, letting it fall free.

"What the hell do you call this?" he asks looking at the holder I had put in my hair earlier that day.

"A scrunchie."

"A what?"

I didn't know how to explain further, so I just remained quiet. Dragon flung the article in question on my night stand. I wanted him, but I needed to hold myself back. I had never in my life reacted to someone the way I did to Dragon. I don't think it's entirely healthy. I need to take a few steps back. That was easier said than done though, because the man of my fantasies was currently undressing.

First the shirt went up and over his head and I found myself staring at his broad chest. It took all I had not to reach up and start licking him like a postage stamp. When his hands went to the snap on his jeans I reach out and stop him.

"What are you doing?"

"Getting undressed babe, it's late and I've got a shit ton of things to do tomorrow."

"You can't sleep naked," I croak.

"I do it every night Nicole. Best you get used to that shit now."

Panic starts to set in, until his words register.

"Umm… why would I need to get used to it?"

"Because babe, you're in my bed. While we're on the subject, cute as that shit is you've got goin' on there, get out of it."

"I'm in your bed?" I asked trying to digest this.

"That's what I said."

"How many others are in your bed?"

Dragon looks at me and it feels like his eyes are boring into me. I did my best to not look away though. I wasn't sure what I was doing or what he was doing. I wasn't even sure what we were doing together! Still, I sensed that this conversation was important.

"Me burying my dick in another woman, I'm sensing is a deal breaker for you."

"Damn straight," I answer immediately.

"Then for however long this lasts, you're the only one who gets my dick."

"You're so romantic."

"Mama if you're trying to mold me into this perfect fucking boyfriend, that's not who I am. I'm dark, I'm jaded and I like my sex dirty. I'm not going to say I'm sorry for being who I am. I like who I am baby, I ain't changing for no fucking body."

I could get pissed here, but the truth was I wanted to have more of Dragon. I had made a decision to live more and I have never felt more alive than when I am around this man.

"Just saying, that if you want to be in my bed, then I want

81

sole ownership of it all, not just your dick—for however long this lasts."

"You're a hard bitch," he said, but he was halfway smiling.

I shrugged.

"Whatever mama, if that's how you want it, that's how you'll get it. Just remember, you are solely mine too. Now strip and get your pretty ass in bed, I'm tired."

I look away as he finishes undressing. It was weird. We've had sex, and I wanted to again. Right now, even. Still, I was embarrassed to see him naked with the harsh light in the room. I walk over to the door and turn out the light. When I turn back around Dragon has pulled the cover down and climbed in the bed. He turns the lamp on that is on the nightstand. He then stretches out against the pillows, his eyes locking on mine, daring me to undress.

I take a deep breath and try to channel my inner Dani. She would have already been undressed and rubbing up against him.

Yes! Yes! Let's do that!

And here I thought Bad Nicole had given up the ghost. I close my eyes, because seriously I couldn't do this any other way. I quickly stepped out of my clothes. I leave my underwear and tank on and climb in the bed.

"You can open your eyes now Mama."

"Um no, I can't, not yet anyways."

"Why the hell not?"

"I have to work up my courage."   Dragon laughs. I had never heard him laugh freely before. It wasn't a full belly laugh, I had a feeling Dragon didn't do those. Still, it was a soft laugh and it warmed me inside. I don't think many people made Dragon do that. I really liked that I could.

He pulled me tight against him. His arm acting like my pillow. He kisses my forehead. I didn't think that was something tough bikers did, but I liked that he did and I wanted more of it.

"Night, Mama," he says softly in the darkness.

"Night, Dragon."

Chapter 10

Dragon

I don't sleep through the night. I can't even remember ever doing that shit. With the life I have led that shit could get you killed, or fucked up in a way that a man wished he was dead. Sometimes the dreams woke me, sometimes the memories, but the point is they always woke me up...except for last night.

I open my eyes up to the sunshine blasting through faded yellow curtains. I never thought much about curtains, especially freaking yellow ones with white daisies all over them. I sure as hell never figured I'd be waking up staring at them. I look around the room and I am immediately bothered. Nicole is nowhere to be found. Damn it, after spending the night curled up against her ass, it did not make me a happy man to find she wasn't nearby. I jump out of bed, not bothering to get dressed. I hear pans banging in the kitchen so I make a beeline for it.

"Not happy Mama."

She turns around to look at me and Christ. She's in her pajamas again, minus those hideous socks she had on last night. Her hair is pulled up and away from her face in another one of those god-awful bun contraptions she had last night. She doesn't have a bit of make up on, and she's in front of the stove holding a spatula and smiling at me. I don't think I have ever seen anything better. Gorgeous! My dick, which had already been hard, now throbbed. Her smile falters and her face heats as she looks at me and takes in my aroused state. So fucking cute! Hell had I ever known a woman who blushed?

"Dragon you're naked!"

"I woke up and my woman wasn't in the bed."

"I was hungry….Wait, your woman?" she asks, but I wasn't in the mood to play twenty fucking questions.

"I was too," I growl, walking over to the stove and turning it off, yanking the spatula out of her hand.

"Was too…what?" she asks, as I put my hands under her ass and pulled her up on my body.

She squeals and then puts her arms around my neck and locks her legs behind my back.

"Hungry," I whisper, nibbling on her neck gently while trying to make my way back up the stairs.

"Holy hell did I enter Skinemax?" a loud voice asks from behind me.

I look over my shoulder to see Nicole's friend standing there. What had Crush said her name was?

I ignore her, more important things on my mind.

"I can't believe you're naked! Dani is ogling your ass!" Nicole whispers in my ear.

Dani, that's her name, whatever. I can't help but grin at Nicole's words though.

"Dani quit staring at Dragon's ass!" she yells, and damn the woman has lungs.

"It's a fucking nice ass Nic. Makes you want to just dig your nails into it and hold on for the ride."

Nicole lays her head down on my shoulder.

"She's not wrong," she sighs, her breath tickling my ear.

My dick leaks at the image of her holding on as I fuck her hard. I want to feel her nails biting into me as her body opens for me to sink into. Aw fuck! If I don't get control I'm going to nail her here on the stairs while her girl is watching.

I count backwards in my head, trying to calm myself. It's hopeless and my control snaps when she begins nibbling on my neck, sucking my skin into her mouth, running her teeth gently against the muscle and releasing with a teasing lick. She has one hand in my hair and another slowly trailing her nails down my chest.

"You taste good Dragon," she whispers, as her fingernails graze my nipple at the exact same time she bites into the lobe of my ear. Nicole's tongue licks over the bite and then twirls in my ear.

I don't know how to explain it. I've fucked so many women in my life, I couldn't tell you who they were, let alone what they looked like. It had always been a warm hole and a way to work out the anger inside of me. You didn't live the life I have led and not be filled with hate and anger. Still, with all the experiences I've had, not one touch had affected me like Nicole's.

I made it to the bedroom, but it was a close call. I slam the bedroom door, drowning out her girls' laughter. I admit I might have run up those last two stairs. I lean against the closed door and let Nicole slide to the floor, keeping her body tight against mine.

"You're running awful hot Nicole after being so cool last night."

"A girl can change her mind, can't she Dragon?" she asks, her voice soft and husky, sending even more need through my body.

"I wasn't complaining Mama, just wondering about my good luck."

"There's something I can reassure you about Dragon," she said.

Nicole pulls away from me and I let her, even though I would rather keep her closer. I was afraid she was going to put a stop to our party and I wish I had kept my damn mouth shut. Instead she shocks the hell out of me and starts taking off her shirt.

"Reassure me?" I ask, watching the shirt fall to the floor, as her hands move to unlatch the front clasp of the hot pink and black bra she's wearing. It's sexy as hell, but can't hold a candle to the way her rose colored nipples are pebbled and her heavy breasts call to me, once she frees them. I make a fist to keep from reaching out and taking what I want. She has a plan and I'm damn sure interested to see where she is going to take it. Still, I have every intention of torturing her later and covering every inch of her breasts with my marks. I want her to look at herself for days and see where my mouth and teeth have been. Fuck, I'm not talking just her tits either. I can't wait to explore her entire body.

"Yeah, because I know beyond a shadow of a doubt, you are going to get very lucky," she says, stepping out of her pajamas to reveal she's not wearing anything underneath. I thought she was perfect in that moment. I honestly didn't believe anything could get better. Then she reaches up, pulls her hair down, and it falls around her face in waves. I drink her in like a man who has been lost in the desert for months. Fucking phenomenal! The fact that her face is heated with embarrassment makes her sexier. She wasn't used to this. She was stepping out of her comfort zone…for me. Opening up and laying herself bare, all for me. I made a decision right there in that moment. It wasn't conscious, it just locked into place. I'd be the last fucking man she opens up to. She was mine and she was fucking staying that way.

"You're fucking gorgeous baby, fucking gorgeous."

Her face heats some more, but she smiles and the nervous worry that had been in her expression left. Some idiot had shaken her in the past. I may have to hunt the fucker down and thank the stupid bastard, after I pound his face in for touching what's mine.

Nicole licks her lips and watching that pink little tongue come out to caress and moisten… shit. I reach for her, but she ignores me. Instead she drops to her knees in front of me. Her hand reaches out and fists my cock, her thumb gently caressing the leaking moisture all over the head. Holy fuck! Those words blast through my mind like a school boy getting his first blow job.

"Do you know what I've wondered Dragon?" she whispers, and I'm looking down to see her staring up at me with her wide blue eyes, and knowing beyond a shadow of a doubt that I am lost to this woman in ways I can't even comprehend.

"What Mama?"

"How you taste… I really want to know. I've been dreaming about it."

"Have you baby?" My voice is shaky as hell and she has me on pins and needles.

I'm waiting to see what she says next, but she surprises me by running her tongue over the head of my cock. She tightens her fist and begins stroking me in a gentle slow rhythm that already has my balls tightening up.

I sift my fingers through her hair. I've never in my life paid attention to color, since too many fucks in my life had shown me a kind of hate, but right now at this very minute it hits me. Her soft, dark blonde hair and darker brown streaks shines bright against my dark skin. As I graze my thumb across her cheek, the pale white of her skin against my darker one is stark, but beautiful. It is completely fucking different, but calls to me. I'm not stupid. I know it has nothing to do with our differences and everything to do with the fact that something inside of me needs this particular woman. Everything about her that I have discovered in the short time I've known her? It soothes me, and is just another reason why I'm not fighting it anymore. My brain screams, *'Mine!'* and I believe it.

As the word echoes in my mind, all thoughts cease at once as Nicole envelops me completely, taking my cock into the hot, wet tunnel her mouth has created. My hand wraps into her hair and my head goes back, as I close my eyes and lose another piece of myself to this woman.

I have to fight to stop myself from thrusting into her mouth, demanding she take what I give her. She started this show and I want her to be the one to finish it. Still she takes me almost completely, her fist stopping me from going too far. Her tongue is darting over the length of my cock, the tight suction of her mouth feeling like heaven. Then her free hand begins palming my balls, rolling them, stroking them at the same time and I know this particular ride is going to end very soon. She moans against my cock and the vibration raises chills along my skin. She's picking up speed, working me harder and faster, harder and faster, and my heart is beating so fast that it may jump out of my chest. I need to stop her. I want to finish inside of her, God I really do, but I don't think I have it in me to pull away from this right now. I need this but I know I should warn her...

"Nicole, God baby…I…I'm…you need to stop…I'm going to come Mama," I rasp out, tightening my fist in her hair to pull her away before it's too late. She looks up at me, her eyes filled with lust, her face flushed, her lips plump and wet. Holy shit I thought she was beautiful before, but now? There are no words. Just her, and she hits me. She hits me all the way to the fucking bone.

"Give it to me Dragon. I want it. Give me every damn drop. It's mine."

Then she plunges her mouth back down over my cock taking every inch I've got to give, like she was starving for it and fuck me I think she is. Whatever this is between us, she's feeling it too. So I stop fighting. I give her what she begged for. My fist wraps tighter in her hair and I fuck her mouth with all I've got, trying to hold on for as long as I can before I explode. I'm holding on until I feel her finger move back to my ass pushing against the opening there and teasing me. There is no holding back after that. One, two, three more thrusts and I cry out her name as I release into her mouth, listening to her moan as she swallows me down.

Nicole slowly releases my cock and the popping noise is loud through the room. She uses the back of her hand and her tongue to clean her mouth but it doesn't seem to bother her. No, she's smiling up at me, and I can't seem to move, barely catching my breath.

"Come here Mama," I growl weakly, because the woman has drained me—in more ways than one.

She stands up gracefully and looks up at me. There's a question in her eyes. I'm not sure what it is, but it's there. I can see some pearl white of my seed on the corner of her lips. I push that into her mouth with my thumb. She sucks my thumb gently, her eyes never leaving mine. I search for something to say. There's something in her eyes and I want to give her what she needs, but I'm a dumb fuck. I've never been here before. My experience with women boils down to get in and get out. Hell until last night, I had never slept with a woman all night. This is completely fucking different for me and I'm at a loss. Still, I want to try, but Nicole stops my thoughts when she smiles at me and says with a dare in her eyes,

"Dragon? I'm not wet."

I look down at her to reassure her that I'm not that man, that she will get her needs taken care of. She takes my larger hand into hers and moves it down between her legs.

"Nicole..." I groan, as I feel how wet the outside of her pussy is, she's drenched.

"This is where you prove I'm lying Dragon," she whispers, moving her tongue over my nipple.

Fuck me, she might be perfect.

Nicole

"Nic! Girl, what the hell did you do with the Twinkies?" Dani asks from behind us.

We're standing in the kitchen. I'm making us some omelets because after round two of Dragon proving why I should probably lie to him more often, we both decided we were starving. Dragon is pushed up against my back, his bare hands stroking my stomach and his semi-erect cock is pushed against my ass. I can feel it, even through his jeans. How he's this ready after the morning we've had is beyond me. The man is insatiable. He has given me more orgasms in our morning together than Tony the Tool gave me during our entire relationship. I'm actually kind of sore from the workout he's given me and it's FANTASTIC! Everything is pretty much in a dreamlike state until Dani's question registers.

My body pulls up taut against Dragon and I look over at the table. Damn I should have cleaned that shit up. I look up at Dragon, who towers over my five foot seven frame. I see mostly his chin at this angle, but I can see the side profile of his face as he takes in the mass destruction of Twinkies. I know he's not going to miss the significance of what I did. He looks down at me and his dark eyes sparkle. THEY FREAKING SPARKLE. Lord. I lick my lips and decide to ignore Dani and Dragon and go back to flipping the ham and cheese omelet.

"Is this a message Mama?" Dragon asks, letting go with one

slow slide of his hand across my stomach and over my side.

"Message?" Dani chimes in. Then her loud laughter can be heard... hell, probably all the way back in Blade.

"I don't find it funny and besides it wasn't a message," I said, grabbing some plates and putting an omelet onto one of them and pouring the ingredients for another into the pan, refusing to turn around.

"What is it then, Mama?" Dragon asked and I gave him a dirty look over my shoulder. He's sprawled out in a kitchen chair in front of the Twinkies, a smashed gooey one in his hand, studying it like it held the secret to life.

"There was a spider," I said defensively, studiously watching my omelet and refusing to look back at him while I tell my lie.

Dani's laughter begins again.

"Holy shit Nic, how big is a spider that causes you to go Thor on a defenseless box of sponge cakes?"

"It was a big spider," I grumble. I take down another plate. "Are you hungry chick?" Maybe food will shut her ass up.

"For your cooking? Always. Now back to this spider."

I flip the omelet into one of the waiting plates, cut it in half and scoop part of it onto Dani's plate.

I turn off the burner and then turn around to look at my ex best friend and the man who may be the best sex I've ever had in my life, but is clearly an ass. I cross my arms above my stomach. I refuse to believe this is a defensive gesture.

"I don't want to discuss the damned spider anymore."

Dragon is studying me quietly, but his face is almost soft. Dani is picking up the mess on the table, every once in a while she'll pick up a poor flattened Twinkie, shake it and then giving me a clearly fake sorrowful look.

"I need to know how big the spider is mama. I might have to have the boys come out and spray," he says so seriously. If I hadn't been watching his eyes and seeing the laughter in them, I would have thought he was being completely serious.

"Twinkies are bad for you," I deadpan.

I hear Dani snort over to my right where she is throwing the damned things into the trash. I wish to God I had done that last night.

"Smooth, Nic," she mumbles, trying to keep from laughing again, and failing.

"Is that right?" Dragon asks, staring right at me. Dani's using a dish cloth now to wipe the table down.

"Yeah it's high in triglycerides."

"Oh Lord," Dani mutters throwing the dish towel toward the sink and hits it perfectly. She then sits in the chair to Dragon's left. To give her credit I can tell she's biting her lip and looking down at the table, to avoid entering into this conversation completely.

"Tryglycer whats?" Dragon asks.

"Triglycerides," I repeat, wishing with all I had in me that I could stop this conversation.

"What exactly are these triglycerides?" Dragon asks and I take Dani's plate and Dragon's to the table to avoid looking at his eyes as I form the lie in my head.

"They…" Shit, what the hell are they? "They're chemicals that are very harmful."

"Is that a fact?" he says, as I put his omelet in front of him.

"Yep! Totally," I confirm with an innocent smile on my face.

Dragon's finger moves up to push some hair behind my ear. It wasn't a sexual move at all, but it made me feel warm inside.

"I actually think I read something about that," Dani chimed in helpfully, as she grabbed the orange juice from the fridge. She brought it to the table and went about getting glasses.

"What kind of things do these chemicals do?" Dragon asked, releasing my hair and looking back at his plate, taking a drink of the juice Dani had put in front of him.

"Do?" I ask panicking, and I am pretty sure he could hear it in my voice.

"Yeah these harmful chemicals what do they do?"

"Umm...they can make your hair fall out." I ignore the sound of Dani choking on her orange juice.

"Well, I've been thinking of shaving my head anyway," he answers quietly, taking a bite of his omelet.

"But I like your hair," I protest without thinking.

Dragon stopped mid bite to smile at me. "Good to know Mama."

I try to keep from sighing. I think I might have failed. I turn to get my food and then join them at the table, hoping this conversation was done. Sadly, Dani didn't seem to want to let it die. I may have to kill her. It's been nice having a best friend.

"I hear they cause crotch rot," Dani chimed in.

I looked down at my own food, suddenly not that hungry. *Crotch Rot?*

"Fuck that'd never happen. I always have my Twinkies while I'm gloved," Dragon said over a mouthful of food.

I thought about what he was saying, and I knew up to and including this point, he had been playing and having a great time doing so. Yet, to just casually throw that out, like it was nothing?

Like sex was insignificant? Then again, he probably thought of it like that. Despite our conversation about it just being me for however long this lasted, I was really nothing to Dragon. For all I know, he means to end it today. I had the image of him with some faceless bimbo in my head and I am starting to get upset all over again. Fuck, I even had unprotected sex with him earlier. OH MY GOD!! It's like I had a death wish. I just opened my legs and let him have his way with me again.

Actually a lot of agains! Seriously Bad Nicole is starting to get on my last nerve.

"Get that out of your head Mama," Dragon growled.

I look up to see him studying me.

"What?" I ask trying to sound innocent and failing miserably.

"Whatever it is that's got you looking all pissed. I've always suited up, you feel me?"

"Not especially. Since I think you might have skipped that step about... oh I don't know, all three times earlier!"

"Three times in a row? I'm thinking I need to find me a big hairy biker to ride," Dani piped up and I flip her off.

Dragon leaned back in his chair and looked at me. I didn't back down. He shook his head.

"You weren't this bitchy with my cock in your mouth. I'm thinking we need to revisit that again."

"Holy fuck me sideways in church and make me scream Jesus! Three times *and* oral sex? Hell, is this a local thing, because damn, I should have moved here when I was fifteen!" I held my head down as Dani chimed in again.

"Bitch please! You were too busy giving it up to Denny Thomas to move," I argue.

"Yeah well, let's just say Denny Thomas did NOT do stamina. Like, at all."

"Not many boys do at fifteen," Dragon points out.

"Did you?" Dani asked.

"I haven't had any complaints."

"I just bet you haven't. Nic, too bad you didn't find 'ol D-Man here before Tony the Tool."

"I need to get dressed," I mumble, giving up all pretense of eating. I stand up taking my plate to the sink.

"Why? I thought you weren't scheduled to work or anything today?" Dani asks.

"I need to drive into town and go to the free clinic," I mutter, wanting away from this conversation, away from Dani and most assuredly away from Dragon.

"What the fuck for Mama?"

I turn around as Dragon's question echoes. He is watching me with a fork full of omelet hovering halfway to his mouth.

"I need to go to the clinic because I've suddenly remembered the side effects of Twinkies."

"And what would that be woman?" he asks, going back to eating. The relaxed vibe coming off of him earlier was completely gone now.

"They pass around germs that can make your dick fall off."

"Good thing you don't have a dick," Dragon returns, the prick.

"You know what I mean!"

"I believe I proved earlier that my dick is more than present and accounted for. I didn't see you complaining about a fucking thing when you were choking on it and begging for more."

Dani stopped eating and looked back at me, quietly

97

whispering, "Oh fuck me…"

She knew me and because she knew me, she knew I was about to blow. "Wrong move D-Man, totally the wrong move."

Dragon didn't acknowledge her. His eyes were hard and they were focused on me. That's okay since I'm pretty sure mine were once again shooting hate rays of death at him.

"Maybe I forgot things I shouldn't have."

"Like what?" he growls, getting up from the table to come over and stand in front of me.

"Okay, so I'll just let you two crazy kids carry on without me. I've got to go pull off my fingernails or stab myself with a dull knife. Anything is more fun than this," Dani says, leaving the room.

"Eyes here Nicole"

Oh *no,* he didn't!

"I'm not a damn dog Dragon, so don't treat me like one."

"Woman you best be explaining yourself, because I thought we had come to an understanding with this shit."

"That's because I was stupid and forgot!"

"Forgot what for Christ sake?"

"That you're a man-whore!"

"Nicole damn it, don't start this shit."

"Start what? You're the one pushing it. I just said I was going to the clinic today!"

"Because you think I'd be stupid enough to pass something on to you. I told your ass I keep my shit gloved!" he growled.

"You say that, but you didn't with me!"

"I didn't hear you telling me to stop and put on a rubber, none of the fucking three times I've been inside you! I sure as hell didn't hear you worrying about shit when you were draining my dick dry!"

"Oh my God! You're unbelievable! News Flash Dragon! Some of that shit can eat through condoms!"

I move to go around him, intent on doing nothing but getting the hell out of Dodge and away from Dragon before I kill him. He wasn't about to let that happen though since he grabs my arm and stops me.

"Don't do this shit Mama. What we got going on, it's good," he said, his voice solid, but quieter.

"I'm getting checked Dragon, and before you put your dick back inside me, you need to go get checked too."

"I don't need this shit. I'm swimming in pussy. I don't need to put up with your tight ass," he says, his voice full of anger.

"Then don't!" I yank on my arm to get away from him. I'm close to tears, but I'll die before he will ever know that.

Instead of letting me go he picks me up and throws me over his shoulder.

"What the fuck are you doing?" I yell, trying to hold onto whatever part of his body I can grab, because it feels like I am falling.

"Mama, I'm going to go wear your ass out so that whatever crawled up in it gets the fuck out of the way."

"Seriously, let me the fuck down!"

"I will as soon as I get your ass back upstairs."

"You know, you pick me up and carry me around a hell of a lot Dragon."

"You complaining, Mama?"

"Hey D-Man you got company!" Dani calls out, when we were halfway up the stairs.

"Probably one of your Twinkies," I grumble.

"Seriously Nicole you need to shut your damn mouth because I'm going to paddle your ass for this shit."

"Yo Dragon, we got trouble man." I look up and get a glimpse of the man who Dragon brought with him to the bar most often, Crusher. Really, who comes up with these names? Dragon swung me around and started going back down the stairs.

"I can walk you know," I whine, because I'm annoyed as hell.

Dragon waited until he got to the bottom of the stairs and then lets me down. Unfortunately, he keeps hold of my hand and drags me behind him to go talk to his buddy.

"Sorry man didn't mean to interrupt. Hey Darlin'," Crush said. His eyes went up and down my body, a little too friendly. I probably should reiterate to Dragon that I wasn't club pussy. Still, I let my eyes travel up his tight and toned body. He was wearing a black muscle shirt, which normally I wasn't a fan of, but he had this sleeve tattoo on his right arm that went all the way up. It was a mixture of blacks and a vibrant red line. It ran along the entire length, twisting and turning all over his arm. It disappears, following his collar bone. I couldn't help but wish he had his shirt off so I could see where else it went and looked like. Not to mention, the way he said Darlin' could make a woman melt. What was it about these bikers?

"Hey," I huff. Dragon's hand tightens up on my wrist and he yanks me so I fall into his side.

"What?" I grouse.

"Quit checking Crush out before I have to kill him," Dragon complains.

My eyes get as big as saucers, because I am pretty sure he's not kidding. I think I can scratch off reiterating not being club pussy off my to-do list.

"Hey boss? Man, we got shit going on. Need you out at Pussy's now."

"OH MY GOD! YOU HAVE A PLACE CALLED PUSSY'S!?"

"It's a strip joint. That's where I was a couple nights ago Nic. Some hot looking women there," Dani chimes in helpfully.

It doesn't surprise me that Dani has been at the strip joint, but I notice the way Crusher checks her out. Men are such pigs.

"Of course it's a strip joint! Dear Lord, I bet you even picked out the name, didn't you Dragon?"

"Shut it Mama."

"This is my home and you can't just tell me to shut up you overgrown..." I stop ranting at him when he reaches down and twists the fuck out of one of my nipples and as a result, I end in a squawk. A squawk that is a painful squeal and an outraged sound of disbelief all rolled into one sound.

Crush gave a half smile, but I could tell he was upset, so I remain quiet. It had nothing to do with Dragon telling me to. Though, to be honest I'm not exactly anxious to have him seek further retribution. That shit hurts.

"What's up?"

"Uh..." Crush looked around the room.

"Speak!" Dragon orders, the man clearly has a big problem with politeness.

"Boss, it's kind of... private."

"Nicole is a part of us now. You feel me? So say what you've got to say or get the fuck out and quit cock blocking me."

I hold my head down. Damn, Dragon has zero filters. I couldn't deny the small thrill I got from him telling one of his boys I will be around for a while. I'm not sure why, but that one sentence paved over some of my insecurities which caused our earlier fight. I wasn't about to tell him that though.

"Boss it's the new girl, Jess. She's been beat up pretty bad. Pops found her out back in the alley."

"Pissed off man?" Dragon asks, and I find myself thinking of this unknown Jess and hoping she would be okay.

"That's just it Boss…she had a note taped on her chest." Crush reached into his inside jacket pocket and handed a folded white paper to Dragon.

Dragon opens the paper and you can see it had been soaked with blood and my stomach twists. That poor girl, what happened to her? I read the note while Dragon stares at it and then wads it up in his hand.

Devil's Fire

I don't know what that means, but from the look on Dragon's face, it's not good.

Dragon looks down at me and he grasps my chin. He looks me in the eye, not allowing me to look anywhere else.

"Mama, I need you at the club. Pack a bag."

"Dragon… I…"

"Mama we got things to discuss. I don't know how long I'll be, but when I get done? I need you there. Yeah?"

"I'll be here. Come here when you're done."

Dragon sighs heavily and I can see in his eyes I disappointed him. When he lets go of my hand, I don't like the feeling that settles in the pit of my stomach.

I reach up and let my hand caress the side of his face.

"Hey, I'll go to the club, just later. It'd take me awhile to get changed and pack. You go do what you have to do and come and get me when you're free."

Dragon looks at me for a minute then nods. I stretch up to leave a chaste kiss on his lips.

"Be careful sweetheart," I whisper and his face changes. I couldn't really describe how, but it was good.

"I like that."

"What?"

"You soft and sweet and calling me sweetheart. I want more of that."

"I'll see what I can do." I smile. Dragon holds my eyes for a minute, and then kisses the freaking hell out of me. I'm still trying to recover when he gives Crusher a nod and they're gone. My stomach is still doing somersaults when the door closes behind them.

Dani is standing over in the corner. I had forgotten all about her. My knees are so weak from the kiss that I had to lean on the furniture to catch my breath.

"Damn Nic. Girl, you might have a problem."

I let out a breath I didn't know I was holding. I had to agree with her.

Dragon

The last fucking thing I wanted to do was leave Nicole. She had become a drug that I was fast becoming addicted to. I had to have more of it, more of her. I had never been in this head space before, especially about a fucking woman and I wasn't sure what to do about it. I just knew I wanted more. I guess comparing a woman to a fucking needle in a fucking vein wasn't what they wanted to hear, but that's what she was. I just left and already wanted another hit.

I have never in my life put a woman before my club or my brothers, but in that moment, I was tempted to tell Crusher to handle shit and leave me with Nicole. I couldn't leave without kissing her. I had to.

When we got to the Pussy Club, all thoughts of Nicole left my mind. Jess was in rough shape. Some fucker had worked her over and beaten her so bad, she was unrecognizable. Her face was swollen and mangled. Her nose was broken and the blood from it ran down and intermingled with what came seeping out from all the cuts on her face. It was enough to fucking turn your stomach. I had seen some fucked up shit in my time, but to know a man had done this damage to a woman? My own stomach churned at the sight.

Poncho, the club doctor who came when we called, had just finished looking her over.

"Fuck Dragon. Someone almost killed this poor slip of a

girl," Poncho said, closing the door and leaving the girl resting on the sofa in the office.

Poncho was a little guy really, standing about 5'. He was skinny and worn out. I wasn't exactly sure how old he was, but I figured him to be in his sixties. Shit though, from the looks of him, he could easily be older. He had been on the Savage payroll since the beginning and even though most of our members had medic training, a doctor was a must at times.

"What damage we talking Doc?" Crusher asked. Shit I was having trouble forming words.

"Her nose and arm are broken, and I can't tell for sure without ex-rays, but I'd say at least three ribs as well, with more bruised. I've reset the nose, taped up the arm tight which will do for tonight. Bring her to the house tomorrow and I'll put her in a cast. I taped her ribs too, but she needs to be watched closely for a while. It's a bad concussion, so I just want to make sure she's okay. Ideally she should be in the hospital, but I know your thoughts on that. I've got Vera staying the night with her and keeping an eye on her vitals."

I nod, wanting to break something but keeping my calm. When I find this motherfucker, heads will roll.

"Anything on the cameras?" I asked Bull, Irish, Crush, and Gunner who had gathered around.

"Fucker took 'em out," Irish spoke up.

That wasn't unexpected, but Bull and I knew something that the others didn't.

Bull had come to me a couple months back, after one of the girls had been having trouble with an ex-boyfriend. The alleyway had been a weak spot in our defenses. As Enforcer of the club, security was Bull's responsibility. Sometimes we ran stuff through the club, sometimes we didn't. I never thought of it before, but this time I was glad. We had decided to install small cameras in areas that were completely unexpected and thus hidden much better. It was fucked up that I had to be happy my brothers didn't know about these cameras. Yet, I was, especially since I was pretty fucking sure what they would reveal.

We had put a series of three cameras along the base of the alley on all sides. They were low to the ground, so they might not show as much as the cameras that had been taken out, but they sure as fuck would show us enough.

Someone was going to a fuck of a lot of trouble to make it look like Skull was trying to start a turf war. So much in fact, they were being obvious, too fucking obvious. I might not like Skull a lot, but he was a smart man and there was no way he'd just paint a neon sign above his head.

"Bull? Have Freak check it."

Irish and the other men looked at me, but I shook my head. I'd talk with my brothers soon.

"Church tonight! Two hours at the shed and every fucking member better be there."

"Prospects too?" Crush asked.

"I got Frog and Nailer watching my woman and her girl. Call Beats and the other newbie out to watch over the rest of the girls here tonight. Close the doors to all the clubs. We're going to go on lock down boys, until this shit is settled."

"Ok Prez," Irish said.

"Your woman?" Crush asks.

Motherfucker.

"Did I stutter?"

"No, was just thinking that sounded pretty permanent Prez."

"My fucking business, you just make sure you respect it."
The warning in my order couldn't be misunderstood.

I trusted my brothers. The original core anyway. But, Crush
had been foaming over my girl too damned much. He frowned
but nodded once. Message fucking received.

Two hours later, I find myself once again staring at my
brothers gathered around this big ass table, and wishing I was
anywhere else. We had been through a lot of shit through the
years. Things others would never experience or know about.
When I say they knew where the fucking bodies were
hidden...they *knew* where the fucking bodies were hidden. I'd
trust every damn one of them with my life. Hell, I had and the
fact I had not one, but two fucking traitors in my club? That was
bitter shit to swallow.

"Where's Striker?" I ask Crush, but knowing now that there
were people I couldn't trust, I feel my gut clench at Striker not
showing.

"Twins said he left the club this morning and hasn't been
back. Not answering his cell, Prez. The boys checked and he's
not at home either."

I nod, but don't say anything. If it was him and the fucker
thinks he can run, he's dreaming. He might run, but he wouldn't
get away. There wasn't a rock big enough for him to hide under.

I nod to Bull, he gets up and locks the door. He stands in
front of it with his arms crossed and waits. Freak gets up next.
He is a scary bastard. He's tall and skinny, but between the tats
all over his body and the many piercings, he intimidates
everyone. That doesn't even take into consideration the bullet
holes tattooed all over his chest and stomach. Screwed up shit.
Stuff looked so real, I had seen them for years and still wanted to

call 911 when I looked at them.

Freak goes to the TV unit on the wall. He puts a disk into the DVD slot on the side. Guess its show time.

Fuck.

I hold the remote in my hand looking down at it and try not to snap it in two.

"Bull came to me a few months back when one of the girls at Pussy's was having trouble with an ex."

"We handled that shit for you Prez," Gunner spoke up.

I nod because they had. Fucker had moved out of state after his beat down. I didn't have a lot of codes I lived by, but a man didn't take his hand to a woman.

This rule was just one reason I'm going to enjoy fucking up the traitors in my club.

"Yeah but Bull and I decided to take other steps," I answer, letting my eyes land briefly on each of my brothers. All of them were pretty cool and calm. One had no reason to be, but I gave him points for having balls. He wouldn't have them long.

Did he have a goddamned clue? Or was he really such a stupid fuck?

I motion to Crusher and Irish and hit play. The screwed up scene unravels as my brothers watch Twist approaching Jess in the alley. Twist jumps up and that's when Irish and Crusher grab him and slam him against the wall. Crusher holds him in place while Irish disposes of his weapons. I walk over to the piece of shit with the sounds of Jess's cries in the background.

"Did you really think you could betray me and my men and survive asshole?"

"Boss you got this all wrong."

I pull out my gun and stick it his mouth.

"Stop your excuses motherfucker," I demand, pushing my 45 into his mouth to shut him the fuck up.

"What you should be doing is begging me to kill you now. It's not going to be that fucking easy for you, though. By the time I'm done with you? You'll beg me to end you. Too bad I won't hear that shit, because after I break your goddamned ass and you sing like a canary? Your tongue will be one of the things I cut off, just for a fucking party."

I hold my hand at Twist's throat and it'd be so easy to snap it and end this pile of dog shit. It's not going to happen though.

"Do you see your mistake yet motherfucker?" I ask, pushing the pistol in his mouth farther and to the right so his head snaps to that direction. On the TV now is a video of Twist just finishing his raping of an unconscious Jess.

"After you finished getting your rocks off on the innocent woman you beat into unconsciousness, you called your fucking partner." I bring my free hand back and punch him in the gut as hard as I can. His groan is muffled by my gun. I pull it out of his mouth and motion to the boys to let go. He sinks down to the floor.

I slam my foot down on his balls and ground my size twelve steel toes even harder just to make sure I've done permanent damage. It doesn't matter, he'll never get a chance to use that shit again. I reach down to grab him by the hair of his head and pull so his face is halfway up to mine.

"Enjoy the pain motherfucker, because believe me, it's just fucking beginning."

Then I take the butt of my 45 and knock the fucker out. Hopefully just enough to make him sleep until we get him moved. I don't want him dead, not yet anyway.

"Get him to the old meat packing plant on the edge of Skull's territory. Time we meet up and discuss what the fuck is going on," I order Bull.

"Yeah Bossman, about that..." Irish interjected, and I look up waiting.

"Frog called. Your woman and that Dani chick are at the movies in Bridgetown. Skull and his crew are there," Irish finishes and I can feel my blood literally boil.

"It appears he didn't take your last warning seriously," Crush says and he had brains enough not to wise crack. He probably knew what a short leash I was on.

"Son of a bitch!" I growl. "Load up!"

Nicole

It had been hours since Dragon had left. Dani and I had gone out and done some shopping in the next town over, just to get out of the house. We ended up at a theater. I made the mistake of letting Dani pick out the movie, and of course we were watching the most horribly overdone freaky ass one ever. It was about a possessed doll, 'Annabelle'.

"Seriously Dani, what kind of twisted freak could come up with this in their head?"

"Quit your bitching girl. Your ass made me watch four fucking hours of Julia Freaking Roberts. Thought I was going to go into barf mode on that last one. I'm just a girl, standing in front of a boy, blah, blah, blah."

I snort. Dani has never, and will never be a rom-com kind of girl. Shit, her philosophy is love 'em and leave 'em before they can screw you over. She has reasons for that though and I understand her. Hell, I'm wondering just how bad the damage with Dragon is going to get. I know it's coming, but I can't keep from wishing he was with me, even now.

"Shhh…" the lady behind us hisses. Seriously, she had been talking on her phone for twenty minutes and she had the nerve to shush me?

"*Amante* Nicole, is that you?" a voice asks from my left, and I know that voice. Oh shit, I just do not have good luck.

The next thing I know, the man Dragon called Skull and five

other men, come over to where Dani and I are sitting. Each one of the men has a woman with them, and a couple of them, more than one.

"Well fuck me Nic, did you start a freaking harem when we moved?"

I sighed. "No, just finding I'm in the wrong place at the wrong time way too much since we moved," I said honestly.

"Do you people mind? We're trying to watch a movie here," Ms. Huffy-phone-woman demands.

"Then watch it bitch." Some skank, and honestly that's what she looked like with her teased out over-dyed blonde hair and fake ass boobs, who was saddled up beside Skull growled.

I push myself down in the seat a little further. "*Mamacita,* does Dragon know you are in my town?"

Dani tilted her head to the side to watch Skull for a minute.

"Your town? Odd, you don't look like a mayor," Dani chimes in.

Skull looks over at Dani and in the darkness of the theater, I could see the white of his teeth show as he smiles at her. I will admit he had a nice smile, and if Dragon hadn't been in the picture, that smile could have melted me. I look over my shoulder to see what it did to Dani. Oh yeah she was melting.

"Yes, well, appearances can be deceiving, can they not, *querida*?" Skull asked.

"That's it, I'm reporting you. I didn't pay my money to miss the movie!" The woman behind us complains and while she's most undoubtedly a bitch, she was also right in complaining. I start to apologize but everyone seems to be ignoring her, so I do too. I have enough pots on the fire, as it is.

"To answer your question, Dragon doesn't really tell me

where I can and can't go. No man does or ever will," I answer easily. I look over at Dani. "I'm going to go get a fresh coke and use the restroom. You want to go?"

"Yeah, sure." Dani knows what I'm doing. We're good at non-verbal communication. I don't know Skull's issues, but I wasn't about to get in the middle of it either.

I start to get up when Skull sits down in the seat beside me, lays his legs out across the top of the seat in front of him and effectively blocks me in.

"Excuse me I was going to the restroom."

"No you weren't, *querida*. You were ditching me, but I am not ready to let you escape."

"Dear Lord Nic, can't you find any normal men?" Dani snorts, turning back to the movie.

"Apparently not," I say with a defeated sigh.

"Skull baby, I thought you and I had plans? Whiny skank pipes up.

The rest of the people with Skull all fell into the row of seats in front of us. It was annoying to watch, but entertaining. They were loud and boisterous, ribbing each other and laughing while annoying every person there. Had I not been desperately trying to think of a way to get away from Skull, I might have enjoyed the show.

Some giant of a man went so far as to pick a woman up and lift her over the top of a seat into the next aisle and place her there. He then did the same to her friend. Skull's crew now had the whole row to themselves. I almost snort out in laughter at the look the women gave back to the big man. I barely contain myself, when the women go running out of the theater.

Dani has no problem letting it hang out though. She cackles

out loudly and throws popcorn at the man in question. He either ignored it or didn't realize what she did. Dani being Dani of course does it again—this time with a handful and most of it meets its mark. He turns around scowling at her and really he was scarier than anything on the screen. I would have backed down and followed those other women out of the theater. That would be the sane thing to do, but not Dani however.

"What's your name big boy?" she asks, as the popcorn bounces on his hair and then falls in front of him.

"Why you askin'," he grumbles and really it was a grumble. His voice was dark, husky and hoarse. It reminded me of a ten pack a day smoker, or a person who has been sick and doesn't use their voice because it hurts to talk.

"I want to know whose name I'm calling out tonight," Dani says with a grin. I hold my head down. I'm used to it of course. My actions in the bar with Dragon were an everyday occurrence to Dani. She made no apologies for it and I admire that. I wish I could be a little more like her at times, but of course even thinking that has heat rising in my face.

"That's Beast," Skull said helpfully. The big man, Beast apparently, turns back around and ignores Dani.

"You're shitting me? Well fuck my ass and pull my hair, I think I'm going to be his Beauty at least for a night or two. Yo! Beast! Turn back around here and let me see those baby blues."

"They're brown," some man beside Beast joins in.

"Well hell I don't care, can't see them anyway, I just want to look at him some more."

"Is your friend always like this, *querida*?"

I look over at Skull, who has a smile on his face. It's dark but I can make out his features, barely. I can't deny he's a good looking man. Still, he didn't make my heart rate ramp up like Dragon.

"Pretty much what you see is what you get with Dani."

"I can appreciate that in people. Can the same be said for you, *querida*?"

"Why are you calling me that, Skull was it?" I ask. He continues to ignore the woman beside him. She huffs her annoyance.

"It is a term of endearment," he responds, reaching over to get some of my popcorn. Skank woman shoots daggers at me and pounces over into the seats with the rest of Skull's people. Really? Like this was my fault? Ugh.

"Help yourself," I grumble, as he put his hands in my food. I hate that. I don't know this guy and I wanted my popcorn, dang it!

"I plan on it, *Mamacita*."

I roll my eyes.

"Give it up, Skull, you haven't got any interest here. You're just trying to one up Dragon."

"And could I? One up Dragon I mean?"

"Afraid not, I can only handle one man on the crazy train at a time."

"A pity, but yet you have not seen what I have to offer, perhaps I may yet entice you."

"You get an A for effort, but don't bother and save us both some trouble."

"I think I might be able to surprise you, *querida*."

I look at him. It's odd because he looks like a macho biker, but smooth businessman in how he talks and that Spanish accent he has? It could make any woman beg and yet, he's doing nothing for me. I look over to Dani, who by this time has climbed into the seat beside Beast and is playing with his shoulder length hair. The fact that the seat she's in is another man's lap doesn't seem to bother Dani. It makes me smile. Beast has no idea what he is in for.

"I don't really know. I just know that as long as Dragon and I are talking, I'm not about to find out," I say honestly, turning my attention back to Skull.

"Dragon is not normally a *uno* type of man, *querida*."

"I don't share."

"He knows this?"

"I don't think you and I need to discuss my relationship with Dragon."

"Fair enough *querida*, fair enough. But I find myself anxious to see Dragon mess up so I can get my shot."

"I think you only want a shot, because Dragon has one."

He smiles but doesn't say anything. An usher comes in and I figure he'd want to tell us to quiet down or kick us out. He takes one look and backs out of the theater. He doesn't even try to quiet Dani and the crew, laughing and making obscene jokes. It would have been a wasted effort anyway.

We all get up to leave when the movie ends. Skull takes my empty popcorn and drink, which he had eaten most of, and tosses them to one of his flunkies. He then pulls me out in front of him. I looked back at Dani who is flirting with Beast, and I have to say, he seems a little more interested. He might not be bad looking, but it was hard to tell between the beard and the long hair.

Skull keeps his hand on my back and guides me through the crowd. I find it odd how I always liked for a man to do that when

I went out, but had never had it. Yet, since meeting Dragon, I'd rather he was here. He wouldn't have a hand at my back. He'd wrap his body around mine and make sure everyone got out of our way.

We make it out into the street when Skull leans down into my ear to talk so he could be heard over Dani and the crew laughing. His hand drops a little too far down so that it is more at the curve of my lower back and ass.

"How about we all go to the Rock, *querida*?"

"The Rock?" I ask looking back at Dani. She was busy now with Beast and the guy whose lap she had sat in. I was feeling uncomfortable. I don't really know what Dragon and I are, but I know he'd hate this.

"It is a club in town. We can have a drink, dance, get to know one another. Your girl seems to be interested in Tiny and Beast."

Shit this wasn't good. I didn't want to ruin things for Dani, but I knew if I went to the club or, hell, anywhere with Skull, then things would not go well. Dragon would flip his lid and he'd have a right to. I took a deep breath and pulled away from Skull.

"Don't think that would be a good idea. Dragon's coming by later and I really should be getting back home."

"Damn straight, Mama."

I close my eyes. Seriously did the man have radar? Dragon and four of his buddies came out of the dark. Dragon's eyes are locked on Skull. He didn't even spare a glance at me, but when his group gets closer, Irish reaches out and puts his arm around my waist and pulls me back against him. Immediately, one of the other men stands in front of me and blocks me from the group.

"Ah, Dragon *mi hermano*, I wondered when you would be

showing up. My *compadres* spotted your man earlier."

"Then you knew to stay the fuck away from my woman," Dragon says. The anger in his voice was so heavy you could feel it.

I hold my head down. Yeah this wasn't going to go well.

Dragon

I don't think I have ever felt jealousy in my life. It just wasn't something I did. Bitches weren't worth the trouble, and that was for damn sure. Seeing my woman standing there though, with another man's hand on her ass, hearing another man ask my woman out? All I knew at that moment, was I wanted to kill. Something violent came out of me at the thought of anyone other than me touching Nicole. I wanted to tear Skull apart limb by limb. Fuck, it was taking every damn thing in me to not do it.

"What the fuck did I tell you Skull? You do not fucking touch her."

"Aw but Nicole…"

"Motherfucker I don't think you're listening. You do not say her goddamn name."

"Surely you do not expect to keep a luscious *mujer* such as Nicole all to yourself?"

I grab him by the neck before he knows what in the hell is going on. I have no plan other than to show this asshole I am not joking and this is no fucking game. I'll gut the motherfucking son of a bitch if he says my woman's name one more fucking time.

"I told you fucker, you do not say her name! You do not even think her name!" I pull my blade out that I keep in my back pocket and hit the button so it pops up. Skull's men go to make a move, but my men circle around. I hear my girl and Dani yelling, but my eyes don't move from Skull.

"I didn't take you for being an *idiota* amigo," I sneer. "Are you? Or are you just eager to sink your dick where I've already been?"

I can hear Nicole in the background. I'm going to pay for that later, but I do not give a damn. Her ass will be so red when I get done with her, she'll be lucky if she can sit for a week.

"Perhaps I have misunderstood *hermano*. I have not known you to be so enamored before. I meant no harm. I will step back if you intend to claim her."

I should let it go at that, but he had his hand on my girl's ass. If it was someone else, I would cut off his fingers and his dick just for fun. If I close my eyes, I can still see his hand there and fuck, I still might.

The rest of my men have come out from the alley where they had been waiting for my signal. We now outnumber Skull's crew easily. He only has a few of his men with him. A mistake, but one I am fucking taking advantage of.

"Tell me Skull, what would you do to a dirty fucker who put his hands on your property?"

Proof that my men know me well, Bull comes around and grabs Skull and holds him for me. Bull's huge ass arms are as big around as a telephone pole. Still, that isn't what keeps Skull from moving. No, that would be the 357 currently cocked and pointing at the side of his head. I take a breath and step back, getting a little space between us now. I need to get a handle on my emotions and tone them the fuck down. Nicole is going to have to learn to stop pushing my damn limits or someone will get killed. I look around and notice that each of my men have a gun trained and aimed at Skull's entourage. They're making sure all our bases are covered.

Nicole's girl and some other bitches are trapped behind Skull's men. The men seem to be protecting them. The guy that was hiding Dani could almost make Bull look small.

"Answer me! What would you do to a dirty motherfucker who thought he could put his hands on your woman?"

Skull, the cocky bastard that he is, ignores the 357 currently pointed at his head and seems unfazed. I could almost respect the motherfucker with his next words.

"I would cut off his hands an inch at a time."

I rub my jaw, feeling the stubble from my five o'clock shadow. I'm pretending to think this shit over. Truth is I may want to, but I'm not going to harm Skull. He needs to stay the fuck away from Nicole, but he is not my problem. No, I was here tonight to chase down what's causing my problems. Skull is a means to that end, because one of my motherfucking problems is locked up in a meat locker on the outskirts of town. One of my own and that shit, even if expected burns in my craw. I turn my attention back to Skull.

"That seems like a plan. I'll start with the fucking hand you had on my woman's ass."

I heard Irish yell out and Nicole hollering back. I turn around to see my boy Irish bent over holding his balls. Nicole comes and stands by me. I blow out a breath and look up at the sky. Fuck, the woman has fire, but she needs to learn when to rein it in. Hell from the looks of Irish, he may never walk straight again, let alone father children.

"Dragon, you are not going to hurt Skull."

"He had his hand on your ass Mama."

Fuck I want to be pissed at her, but she looks so fucking

sexy standing there in those tight ass jeans and blue sweater. That sweater is molded to those fucking breasts of hers and her hair is all messed up from wrestling with Irish. My cock instantly reacts, damn thing stays hard if she is anywhere around.

"Yes well, we were discussing that."

"What's to discuss Mama? He had his hand on your ass. Did you want his hand on you woman?"

"Don't be stupid," she growls at me, and I somehow keep from smiling as she berates me in front of my men. What the fuck has she done to me?

"You and me, what we got going on? You're mine. That means his hands or any other fucker's hands better not touch you."

I expected her to argue, fully expected it. The fact that she didn't, calms me as nothing else would. Instead of arguing, she comes closer and wraps her arm around me. Does she know what she just agreed to, in front of everyone? Does she have any idea she sealed her fate right here in this moment?

"He's sorry Dragon. He was just about to apologize."

All the men start laughing. With her acceptance of my claim the tension seems to lessen around the group.

"I'm actually not that sorry *querida*. It was worth it."

"Will you shut up? Do you want him to kill you? Perhaps it has escaped your notice that there's a man pointing a gun at your head!" Nicole snaps.

I look at my girl and grab the back of her neck and pull her close. She squeaks, but she doesn't fight me. I lean down so our foreheads touch. Her blue eyes are so fucking deep, I could drown.

"Shut it, Mama."

"You can't hurt him Dragon."

"Why's that?"

"I'd miss you if you went to prison."

"You could visit me."

"I don't date men who wear orange. It's a rule."

Fucking cute.

"Kiss me Mama."

"Dragon we're on the street with a hundred people and guns are involved. I don't think now is the time to kiss," she argues.

"You can give me your lips or I can always cut off Sku...." Her lips press against mine, cutting off the rest of my words. Her tongue pushes against my lips and I open immediately, taking control. Our tongues fight and duel with one another and when I finally pull away, she sighs and lays her head on my chest.

"Are we going to have trouble?" I ask Skull. He looks down at Nicole with a look of want on his face, but I'm good at reading people. It's not exactly Nicole he wants, but what she's giving me. I don't like it, but I understand it. Totally, but I'm not letting this slide through my fingers. Life has been shit mostly. Nicole deserves better, but they'd have to fucking kill me to get her away from me at this point.

"We're good. Call off your men, *mi hermano*. You are a lucky son of a bitch, Dragon. She's a hot..."

Smarmy motherfucker! I twist away from Nicole and nail him in the ribs with a hard right.

"Respect my woman and keep your fucking distance brother," I sneer.

Skull bends over with a groan as my punch is delivered. I had claimed Nicole. I never imagined doing that shit with anyone before, but if I'm going to do it, then it better damn well be respected.

"Tomorrow night around nine, have your men at the old butchering plant. Watch your backs," I order Skull.

He was rubbing his ribs, watching me, and I could see anger there, but something more. Skull and I understood each other.

Chapter 15

Nicole

I could possibly be insane. I was in a whirlwind relationship with a man, I honestly barely knew. It seemed surreal. I was terrified. I don't think it's supposed to happen this fast. What if I'm making the worst decision in my life?

The thing is, when I am with Dragon, it doesn't feel wrong. It feels as if everything is right. Dani thinks I'm insane. She's pissed I left with Dragon tonight. She went with Skull's crew to the bar. I personally think she's the one asking for trouble, but unlike her, I'm not going to bitch at her about it. I pick up my phone and text her one last time.

Let me know you're ok. Be safe. N

I stare at my phone waiting for her to reply. I know no matter how pissed she is, that she will answer. It doesn't take long.

Go back to putting your nose in Dragon's ass mom. I'm fine. L8r.

Yep she's still pissed. I sigh and throw my phone over on the nightstand. Dragon comes out of the bathroom with a towel around his hips. Lord he's fine. It's no wonder things have moved so fast. A woman would be out of her mind not to try and hold on to a piece of that.

"What's that look for Mama?"

"Dani's still pissed."

Dragon walks to the left side of the bed, which he had

claimed as his the last time. He takes the towel off, lays down and pulls me against him. He smells of soap and rugged man and another scent I couldn't define that was just him. I snuggle in and enjoy.

"Dragon, I think I'm getting addicted to you," I say, my eyes drifting closed as his hands sift through my hair.

"Good," he responds as I kiss his chest.

"Dani might be right. We've only just met and it *is* a little crazy how intense we are."

"You women think everything to death. We're fucking, it's good. We both want more, end of story."

"You would be every woman's wet dream if you didn't open your mouth."

Dragon laughs and it is a nice sound, so I try to concentrate on it and not the fact that I want to slap him. Did he realize what he said? He went crazy when Skull casually touched me. That's not a reaction to have about a girl you're just fucking, is it? Hell, maybe it's different for a man. I have no idea.

"Is that what we are Dragon? Two people fucking?"

"Hell I don't know Mama, we are what we are."

I roll over onto my back. I don't know what I expected, but somehow I know it wasn't this. Dragon turns to face me, his rough finger slowly tracing an imaginary line along the side of my face.

"What's going on in that mind of yours Mama?"

"I don't know how to do this Dragon. I don't know what we are…What I am to you?"

Lord I sounded pathetic, but I had made the decision to take the leap, and he was making me feel like I was standing on a piece of ice that was quickly melting. I close my eyes and concentrate on his touch, letting it center me.

"You're mine. Every fucking inch of you is mine," Dragon said, pulling the covers off of me. "Oh Mama, you got into the bed naked. You're being my good girl tonight."

I gasp as the cold air hits my body and his rough callused hand moves over one of my breasts.

"It seemed like it would be a wasted effort with you."

"Damn straight. Do you want my mouth or my cock?" he asks, and really is that even a question?

My hips thrust up as I watch him take two of his fingers and move them around my pussy, swirling them in the wetness he found there. I can feel his thumb come up and press hard against my clit as his fingers slowly move in and out. Phenomenal!

"Tell me which one does my woman want?"

"Oh God, both Dragon, give me both," I moan, bringing my legs up trying to take his fingers in deeper.

"Such a greedy bitch," he growls in my ear.

He moves down my body, the roughness of his hands leaving a blazing trail behind. What he does to me is beyond words, it is fucking perfect. I never knew it could feel like this.

"My baby wants me to eat her pussy?"

I was beyond answering by this point. My eyes close, my head pushes back into the pillows, as his hot breath caresses my folds.

I thought I was prepared, but I'm not sure anything could have prepared me for what came next. He grabs my hips and pulls my pussy to him.

There's slow and steady and then there is Dragon. He attacks me. There's no slow build up as his tongue plows into me, sliding over my folds and pushing inside of me.

My hands move down to grab his hair and pull him closer to me. I thought it couldn't get any better and then his tongue moves and teases me in all the delicious spots that I swear I don't think a man before him had ever touched. He bites down on my clit, not hard but with just enough pressure every muscle in my body tightens up as if I am walking on a tightrope.

"Dragon...," I gasp. Hell my eyes might have rolled back into my head.

He lets go and stretches me with another finger while at the same time licking along the swollen nub he had just seconds ago, captured between his teeth.

I grind down on him, going out of my mind. I want him to hit that spot, I crave it. I'm pretty sure no one would ever be able to hit that spot but him.

I tighten my inner muscles around his fingers bucking and riding, knowing I am close to exploding. I pull his head into me as hard as I can when he moves his tongue over and over my clit while finger fucking me at the same time. I am so close to my orgasm I can literally taste it. When he pulls away, I cry out in disappointment.

He smiles down at me, his fingers still inside of me, but refusing to move. His face is wet with my cream and his eyes have this heavy slumbered look about them. My pussy spasms at how masterful he looks at this moment.

"Want to come baby?" he asks, his cocky voice should have annoyed me, but it didn't. It made me hotter.

"Please....," I whimper. My hips thrusting up because he's refusing to move and I need it. God I need it.

"Who owns this pussy, Nicole?"

I moan as he times a thrust of his fingers with the question.

He is killing me.

"Answer me woman! I asked you, who owns this fucking gorgeous pussy?"

"Dragon…" Again he strokes me hard in time with his question.

My eyes are closed and I'm waiting for the explosion I know he is building. He flicks his finger back and forth over my clit and then dives in with his tongue. He stiffens his tongue and somehow uses it in tandem with his fingers and my whole body begins to quake.

I whimper in disappointment when he pulls away again. I am so close.

Dragon has other plans though as he reaches over me and takes my hand and pushes two of my fingers into my mouth.

"Lick on them fucking fingers Mama. Suck them into that hot little mouth of yours like it's my cock you're sucking."

I couldn't disobey him even if I wanted too. I lick and suck on my fingers. My eyes open halfway so I can watch him as I do what he orders.

"Now use them to tease your nipples Mama. Pull hard enough you feel that bite of pain and show me what a dirty little girl you are."

I do as he instructs. His fingers are moving slow and steady back and forth inside of me. Hell, as long as he keeps that up, I'll do anything he wants. My fingers roll my nipples between them, the wetness making them slide and causing a delicious friction. I pull until I feel the edge of pain, causing my clit to throb harder. A moan escapes and I dig the heels of my feet deeper into the mattress, wanting his fingers deeper inside of me.

"Oh fuck yeah, that's it Mama. I love watching you play

with your tits. So fucking hot, I'm about to explode all over you."

My eyes lock on him, refusing to leave. He pushes his own finger into my mouth now, without saying a word. I keep my eyes open, my hips rocking in the gentle rhythm he has started.

"Suck."

Just that one word, ordered out of his gravelly aroused voice and I'm so close to exploding, I'm not sure I can hang on. I move my tongue over his finger, sucking like it's his cock, which is what I really want right now.

"Yeah Mama that's it, my woman likes it don't she? Take that finger like it's my cock you're devouring. Show me that dirty little girl I know is inside of you."

I've never been like this. Sex was decent before Dragon, but nothing like this. Never had a man talked so much during sex and the frank talk and plain spoken words make me hotter than I have ever been. He pulls his finger away slowly and I instantly miss it.

"You're mine now Nicole. I own your hot little mouth," he says. He bends down and pushes his tongue into my eager mouth. I am on fire. My tongue tries to reach everywhere, to drink him in completely. Just when I think I might succeed, he pulls away.

"I like having the taste of your pussy on my mouth when I kiss you," he whispers, straightening back up.

"I own this sweet little cunt," he says moving his fingers just a little. It's enough to make my hips thrust though. "I own this whole fucking body now and I'm never letting it go. You hear me Mama?"

God, I did hear him and my heart stalled and then took flight at the thought of what he was saying. I couldn't concentrate though, because at that moment he takes the finger I had been sucking on and pushes it against my ass, sliding it slowly into the opening. I tense up. I had never gone there before. I had been curious, but the two lovers I had didn't exactly inspire me to try new things.

Dragon eases his finger inside, while gently moving the fingers he already had inside my pussy. My ass was at an angle now, lying half way on his lap my legs spread, so that one was on each side of him.

"Fuck yeah, take my finger inside that tight little ass. I'm going to fuck you here soon Mama. Push my dick in you and fuck you so hard you'll have my balls spanking your pussy with each thrust."

"Dragon... oh God I'm...I'm getting close baby," I moan out... at least I think I do. Everything is starting to blur. I can feel my orgasm approaching and I know it's going to be huge.

"You ever been fucked here Nicole?" he growls, his finger sliding further into my ass while his other fingers curl up. He is getting so close to what my body needs, the wait is killing me.

I moan out trying to tighten myself up around his fingers, thrusting in no rhythm at all, just trying like crazy to get what I needed.

"Answer me woman and I'll give you what you want," he demands and our eyes lock.

"No."

"It's mine. No other fucker gets that from you but me Nicole. No other man touches you again," he growls, and I can do nothing but nod in agreement.

"The words Nicole, say them."

"No one but you Dragon," I say without hesitation, because I know in my heart that this is what I want. This is what I've wanted from the first time I laid eyes on him.

His eyes go darker than midnight, his face so intense I blink to see if it will change. That look, the emotions on his face, this is why he is called Dragon. It feels as if he's going to burn me alive with the heat coming from him at that moment.

He increases the thrusts of his fingers, his eyes glued to my body, watching as he works me. I cry out, knowing I'm lost and not able to hold it back.

It explodes as I scream out his name. I try to twist and turn to get away from him. The feelings are so intense, so cataclysmic I think it may kill me. Dragon allows me no mercy. He pushes harder on my clit, not allowing me to escape. I whimper as the vibrations in my body don't get a chance to settle completely down before they start again. His fingers move harder, faster and his growl echoes in the room.

"That's it Mama. So fucking beautiful, watch that little pussy begging for everything I can give it. I'm goin' to fuck you so hard in a minute, just as soon as you come for me again."

God, his words set me on fire and I feel my climax building. Just as I start to explode, Dragon takes his hands away.

"No damn you, don't leave!" I demand and Dragon laughs. I'd cuss him but at that exact moment his cock plunges into me and his thumb pushes down on my clit.

"Oh fuck!" I holler or he does, hell maybe we say it together. I'm trying to hold on because seriously, a woman could pass out from everything coming at me and I don't want to miss a moment of this.

"So fucking perfect. I'm going to fuck this pussy so hard and so often, so you know there's no one else out there for you, but me."

"Never anyone but you," I pledge, barely coherent.

"Damn straight Mama. Fuck, I'm so close. Come again baby, come all over my cock and take me with you."

I moan because now speech is beyond me. He does something with his fingers on my clit. I have no idea what, all I know is it shatters me. I detonate on a wild cry. It takes just a minute more and I feel Dragon explode inside of me.

He's ruined me for other men. That thought drifts through my mind as I feel him move to the side and pull my boneless body close to him. He is running his fingers through my hair. It's such an odd thing, him doing that. Seems out of character with the big bad biker persona he has going on.

"I want you at the club tomorrow. You'll move into my room with me."

"You live at the club?" I ask, realizing Dragon and I are really just getting to know each other.

"Yeah, I've never had reason not to. Club is on lockdown though, so I need you with me."

"Lockdown?"

"Yeah Mama, got shit going down so I need to know you're where me or my boys can protect you."

"Does this happen often?"

"Not often, but it does."

"I'm not part of the club, I don't see why I'd need to be there."

"Because you're mine, I've claimed you and they can use you to get to me."

I guess that makes sense, didn't mean I liked it though.

"You need to learn better post-copulation talk Dragon."

He reaches down and kisses the top of my head, with a snort.

"Post copulation? You gonna get fancy with me Mama?"

"I do kind of feel like royalty tonight."

"Is that a fact?"

"Well you did worship my body," I giggle.

"You want to clean up Mama and I'll give you more reason to feel worshipped?"

"I kind of like the feeling of having a part of you inside of me...dripping and sliding between my legs..."

"Fuck me. I thought I was done, but suddenly I want to feel that too."

"About time."

"I'm going to have to tame you before you kill me," Dragon said climbing back on top of me. I look into those dark eyes, they never fail to stop my heart.

"Bring it on, Big Boy."

And he did.

Chapter 16

Dragon

Fuck it had been a stressful two days. I finally got Nicole packed up and moved into the club. She was fighting me with every breath, mainly because her girl was being a bitch and was refusing to come with her. Nicole had flat out refused until I got a little more creative with my convincing.

Tonight would be the first real night Nicole would be staying at the club. I wasn't going to fucking lie, I didn't know how she was going to fit in. I was expecting drama with the Twinkies. Tonight was also a party night, and Nicole would probably see shit that would   make her run. I wouldn't let that happen. At least I was going to try for that to not happen, but then Skull had canceled out our meeting the night before and we were meeting up tonight instead. I was fucked. I couldn't be there watching over my woman and here with my men and Skull at the same time, and I fucking needed to be here.

Crush and I walked into the old factory's slaughter room. I normally took care of my business at the shed, but since this involved Skull to a certain extent, I moved to a more central location. I didn't like it, but I also didn't want that fucker on my turf, knowing where my shit was.

Skull and three of his men, Beast, Copper and Torch, were already sitting in the corner watching as Gunner was hosing down our entertainment for the night. Bull and Freak were sitting across from Skull's men saying nothing, just watching. I had

Irish, Frog and Striker watching over my woman. I was still hesitant about Striker, but he seemed to be innocent of this shit. I couldn't go around blindly accusing all of my own men. With three of them there, surely Nicole would be safe. That's all I could do for now and it's the only way I would agree to come here tonight.

Twist had been tied up on a meat hook now for two days. His face was swollen, his ribs bruised and I could tell Freak had been working on him with his razors. There were fine little lines with blood trailing along them all over Twist's naked body. The lines were cut just deep enough to separate the layers of skin, and in perfect vertical form, straight as an arrow, except for the word 'Rapist' that was written across Twist's stomach. Freak was an artist with a knife or razor. He was a scary fucker, but handy to have on your side for damn sure.

"Let's get this damn meeting started," I said, as I sat down at the table across from Skull.

"Damn Dragon, I was hoping the lovely Nicole had improved your mood."

"She did, that's why I want to be done with this shit and get back to her."

Skull was wise enough not to say anything back. Good call.

"My boys explain shit to you?"

"*Si*, though I am sure you know by calling this meeting, I am not so stupid as to leave a clear trail pointing back to me or my *compadres*," Skull answered.

"I do, which means we both have an enemy we need to find before this shit escalates."

And fuck me, but this shit always had a way of escalating. It hadn't bothered me before, but now I had Nicole to worry about.

I still wasn't sure how the hell that had happened.

"Freak, you about ready to start?"

"Plastic is all rolled out just waiting on you Bossman," he said as if he was bored.

I look at Skull. "You warned me about this motherfucker before. Do you have any more intel you're willing to share?"

"Sorry *mi amigo*, I wish I did, but I have nothing I wish to speak of to you or your compatriots"

Fuck! That meant he knew something more, though nothing he was willing to tell me. Why can't shit ever be simple?

I rake my hand over my head. I dread what's coming next. I can handle beating down and torturing motherfuckers, especially when they bought their own ticket. In my world you had to prove you were strong. You had to be someone others could not fuck with.

Still, the fact that tonight I would be doing that shit to one of my own was bitter in my gut. I keep my mind on Jess. It replays the beat down Twist gave her and how he laughed with each kick of his steel toed boot. It pictures how he raped the poor unconscious girl afterwards. Jess was a sweet girl, and looking at her, she even reminded me a little of Nicole. I kept that thought up front as I got up from the table. I make my way over to Twist and remind myself that this fucker destroyed an innocent woman and betrayed his brothers. Gunner turns off the hose.

"Untie him and put him in the tub. You got the shit on?" I ask, because there's not a doubt in my mind how this is going to go down.

"Yeah, Danny has the stuff going now."

I nod and stand against the wall watching as Freak and Gunner lower Twist into the cast iron tub. His eyes are swollen together so he can't see, but he has to know what's happening. He's seen what we do to those who betray and try to cross us. There's a reason we're the Savage MC. I grab the pliers and knife off a makeshift table and walk towards him.

Truth be told, I don't have a stomach for this shit. This was only done when information was needed. I'd much rather shoot a fucker between the eyes than go through this. I know my men felt the same. Freak took care of the crap job, because it had to be done and done right, to protect the club. I knew he didn't truly like it either. Fuck, if he did I'm not sure I'd want him on my side.

I bend down and take the filthy oiled rag from his mouth that the boys had used to gag him with.

"You ready to talk fucker?" I ask, already figuring what the answer would be.

"Fuck you. You're going to kill me anyway," Twist said, and let's face it, he wasn't wrong.

I grab him by the hair of the head and decided to lay it out for him.

"There is a world of difference in how you die. I can make it easy, I can make it hard. Now, I know what I hope you'll choose, but betraying the MC shows me you're not the brightest fuck. So, I figure you might need some convincing."

"I'm not telling you a thing," Twist rasps, and I pull over the small stool by the tub to sit on. I was right, he's not that bright and obviously this is going to take a while.

"Do you know what lye is fuckwad? See everyone talks about acid, but if you heat lye up way past boiling and pour that shit on a human body? In just a few hours all you got is liquid slop," I tell him, as I run my Bowie knife along the outline of his

Savage MC tat on his chest. All the brothers had one and clearly I needed to be more careful about who I let wear it.

This fuck up was on me. I knew I should have blackballed Twist from the beginning, but Irish, Gunner and Striker had all voted to patch him in. I usually tried to run the club by majority vote. This was one time I should've paid attention to my gut.

"We've used it before. Fuck, stinks worse than pigs in shit. There won't be a trace of you left for one sorry-ass to grieve. It'll be like you never existed. All we do is pull the drain open and wash you down into the sewers where shit like you belongs."

"Fuck you," Twist replies back, but oh I can hear the fear in his voice this time. That was good, because fear meant the fucker might tell me what I needed to know.

"What really bothers me the most is that none of the other punks who tried to betray the MC held our mark on their chest."

"Yo, Crusher! You think we should allow Twist to carry our symbol on him into hell?" I ask, my knife still dancing around the tat in question over the heart.

"Abso-fucking-lutely not, Prez!"

"Yeah, I don't think so either, but let's be fair. All those that say this fuckwad can keep his tat, say Aye."

I reach over and put on the latex gloves that Freak had put on the floor beside me. I waited a minute for effect and then lean even further down so my voice is in Twist's ear.

"Listen to that silence, fucker. Looks like fun time is about to begin."

Then I let my knife slice into the skin in a deep X through the tattoo. I pick up one of the loose pieces of skin and saw it off, throwing it into the tub. I do that four more times until the tat is removed and the pieces are lying along Twist's naked legs.

Twist had screamed and is crying now, but I block that shit out. I'm sure Jess cried out too, and she was just a helpless slip of a thing. Twist deserves this and worse. I lay my knife on a rag that has been placed on the floor and then take off my bloodied gloves, throwing them in the tub.

"I swear you might be more of a pussy than I thought Twist. You're crying more than poor Jess did. Did it make you feel like a big man hurting someone innocent? To rape a woman you had already beaten to the point she was unconscious?"

I picked up the pliers and twisted the fuckers head back.

"Danny told me his stew manages to melt everything but you know me Twist, better to be safe than sorry. Hold still now, this is going to hurt like a son of a bitch. Kind of like how poor Jess felt when you broke her fucking arm," I said, using my pliers to rip out one of his front teeth.

"Or maybe it will hurt as much as when you broke three of her fucking ribs you ass fuck."

I put the tooth on the plastic by my feet and yank out two more. Twist is trying to moan but since I kept the pliers jabbed into his mouth that's pretty much impossible.

"Shit boys, Twist smells like he's been sucking your dicks. Damn breath is killing me," I complain, going in to pull another one. Twist passes out and I put the new tooth with the other three. Then yank off the new set of gloves I had put on, throwing them in the tub.

"I'm taking a break. Wake the fucker up in a bit and get him ready for round two," I growl walking to the door. "Skull, you and me now," I order, and didn't look back.

I light a cigarette and lean up against the outer wall of the building, waiting for Skull. He didn't take long and I offered him a smoke. I didn't usually smoke, but some things called for a good smoke and a stiff drink. Fuck if this wasn't one of them, I may even let myself get lost in the booze later tonight.

"It is not easy being a leader *mi amigo*," Skull said, taking a smoke and looking out over the abandoned property.

The cement is cracked and weeds are growing through it. There are a couple of old junked cars and lots of trash. Place is a shit hole, but with the purpose it serves, that seemed fitting.

"What aren't you telling me, Skull?" I ask straight out. It is time to cut the bullshit. Skull and I would never be the best of friends, but there is a grudging respect of sorts.

He takes a drag on his cigarette and blows out the smoke. In the distance a train whistle lets out a lonely wail.

"Dragon, talk on the street is of two adders in your nest, *mi amigo*. The fuck up in there being a small fry in a big ocean, and word is trouble is headed your way."

"Trouble is headed my way every damn day," I growl, watching the glow of the fire burn on the butt of my cigarette.

"Perhaps."

"Besides, I already knew that shit from the call Twist made at the end of the tape, asking if I was distracted."

"*Si.*"

"So, you have names?"

"None I am willing to share at this time, but I will when I find a reliable source. Doing so now may implicate an innocent man. I warn you though, you shouldn't trust anyone."

I threw the cigarette away and gave Skull a hateful look. I might understand what the fuck he was about, didn't mean I had to like it.

"Let's get this shit done."

Chapter 17

Dragon

It had been a fucked up day. I had pulled the rest of Twist's teeth and cut off his fingers, when it became apparent the fucker wasn't going to talk. It pissed me the hell off. I needed something more to go on and for some reason I thought for sure Twist would have caved. All he would tell me in the end was that he'd see me in hell. A man could almost respect that, if it hadn't come out of the mouth of a woman beating, rapist.

I don't know why he didn't break. Whoever was behind this shit, cultivated a fuck of a lot of loyalty apparently. I had left Freak and Gunner to deal with what was left of the scum. There wasn't much left though. The skin with the fingerprints and the teeth were dissolved separately, so I could be sure there was nothing left. Then the Mexican stew Danny had prepared was poured into the tub with Twist. It took several hours, but eventually he really would just be a stain in a sewage line. The fucker deserved less than that.

Now I'm sitting here at the club getting drunk. Nicole had come over and tried to pull me out of my head several times, but I shot her down. Why? Because I'm a fucking asshole, that's why. She doesn't deserve it, and I can tell from the blush on her face I had embarrassed her.

Now, she is watching the club Twinkies and she is clearly not happy with what is going on. I hated to tell her, but for the most part this was a quiet night for everyone. Hell, there wasn't even any open fucking going on. That will probably change before long, since the alcohol is flowing heavily and all of my men are in fucked up moods.

Nicole is at the bar talking with Lips and Irish. It's kind of odd how her and Lips seem to have hit it off, but they are laughing as if they are old friends. It kind of pisses me off, though I cannot tell you for the life of me why.

Irish keeps looking over at me, giving me a strange look and then shaking his head.

Yeah well, I know I'm fucking up so what, I say to myself, as I raise my glass to him in a silent toast. Irish shakes his head and goes back to talking to the girls.

Nicole shoots a worried glance in my direction every now and then and I do my best to ignore the pleading look in her eyes and keep drinking. I had nearly finished the bottle when Tash comes over and sits in my lap. I didn't want her there. I might be fucked up right now, but even in this state, I knew Nicole was all I wanted. I am about to push her away when I hear Nicole's voice. I look up to see my woman walking toward us in an angry strut, so fast her hair was flying behind her like there was a breeze and it bounces on her shoulders with ever step. Fuck, she is magnificent. I close my eyes and remember the way she had looked sucking on my cock. I instantly go hard, which considering the amount of alcohol I had been drinking, is no small feat.

"You need to move your boney ass off my man's lap."

My brain was mush, I should be paying attention to what the women are saying, but in truth all I could watch was the swell of Nicole's breasts rise and fall in the sweater she was wearing. The deep V-neck of the dark green sweater gives a great view.

"I don't see your man complaining. Maybe you just can't keep him satisfied like I do."

"Bitch, I'm telling you one last time to step the fuck away," Nicole growls.

Tash turns around and plants her lips on mine and pushes her tongue into my mouth. I bring my hands up to her shoulders to push her away but I never get the chance. I hear Tash scream. Then, she is off me and Nicole has pulled her onto the floor. I shake my head to clear it. When my vision improves I see Nicole with Tash's hair in her hand pulling her away from me. Tash is probably a good three inches taller than Nicole, but apparently that doesn't matter when anger is involved. Well that and the way Nicole has the woman's hair pulled so tight her head was bent all the way back. She has Tash bowing down to try and get her hair loose.

"Mama...." I start and shit, my voice even sounds slurred to my own ears.

"Don't you fucking start right now, me and this bitch have something to clear up. You said I was your woman, is that still true?"

"Fuck yeah," I tell her, because my head wasn't so foggy I was completely stupid.

"You hear that bitch? That means he's mine because I don't fucking share. I warned your fucking ass before you came over here, but I see the peroxide has melted what few brain cells you had. Stay away from my man," she yells! She then slams Tash's face down on the table so hard, I thought it might crack.

Fuck! I wince at the thought of the pain that had to have brought. At the same time my dick pulses. Hell, I had been afraid Nicole wouldn't be hard enough to stand up for herself, I had no idea.

Tash sinks down onto the floor with a low moan, her nose is at a weird angle and there is blood coming from it. Nicole kicks her once more for good measure before she steps back. Everyone is staring at her and my woman stares every single fucking one of them down.

"Anyone else want to try and touch what's mine?"

Silence.

She looks back at me and the hurt and anger in her eyes are almost enough to sober me up.

"I don't know what the fuck is going on with you Dragon, but I don't play these games. If you want this shit take it, but don't think I'll be sitting back and waiting. I told you in the beginning, I don't share. Now since you smell like some other fucking bitch's cheap ass perfume, I'm going back home."

She stomps away from me and I watch her for a minute. I mean I think I am in shock and at the same time she is so fucking hot with that plump ass in those tight jeans. Her sweater had risen up and I get a peek of the curve of her ass as she walks.

"Nicole!"

She stops as she gets to the door.

"I think she touched my back. Could probably use some help washing that shit off Mama."

I need to be tougher and make sure the men see me as strong, but right now in this moment, I don't give a fuck about anyone or anything other than Nicole.

The twins have pulled a dazed Tash away, but other than that there's no movement. Everyone is waiting to see how this plays out.

Nicole turns and looks at me, her eyes appraising me and I

get the feeling she sees more than anyone else ever has. Then again, I don't think anyone has really given a shit before. They sure as hell had never claimed me as theirs, like this woman had done just moments before.

I watch her slowly walk back towards me. With each step she makes, somehow the heavy load that had been on my shoulders since doing all that shit to Twist, gets lighter.

She stops in front of me and I know beyond a shadow of a doubt I have never seen anything more beautiful. I was in fucking deep with this woman.

She holds out her hand and I take it. We walk back to my room. Fuck, it is our room. I need to start admitting I'm never letting her go.

The sounds of the party slowly begin to pick up in the background.

When we make it to the room I close the door and lock it. Nicole goes to the shower and turns the water on.

I pull my shirt off and throw it on the floor, following her.

I remain silent, kicking my shoes off. Nicole apparently knew I couldn't talk. I don't know why that surprises me but it is becoming clear that this woman gets me. It is a fucking strange feeling.

"You pull this shit again Dragon and I walk," she says. I don't bother responding since she is undoing my pants.

I step out of my clothes and stand in front of her naked. A fine red heat spreads over her face and it amazes me. This woman, who had only moments before stood in front of a rowdy bunch of strangers and went toe to toe with some of them, while at the same time claiming someone like me as her own, blushes just from looking at me naked.

"Mama, you have too many clothes on," I complain. Earlier my head was foggy from all the rot gut I had consumed but I feel mostly sober now. Still buzzed, no doubt about that, but completely aware.

I watch as Nicole pulls her sweater over her head and kicks off the sandals she had been wearing. Her breasts are confined in a blue silk bra and almost falling out of it. She leaves the bra on and slowly peels her pants down her body. She stands before me in nothing but her matching underwear and it hits me again how perfect she is.

He's mine.

I hear her say it over and over in my head.

"God Mama, you are so fucking beautiful you make me ache." I feel my balls tighten and my cock grow harder than it has ever been before. I stroke it slowly.

Nicole watches me stroke myself and I can tell she likes it. Her eyes take on a slumberous look she gets when she is turned on. Her hands shake softly when she reaches up to pull her bra straps down off her shoulders.

She bites her lip and unhooks the clasp on her bra that is resting between her breasts.

Her eyes follow my thumb as I move my pre-cum back and forth over the head of my cock, stopping only to stroke. She pulls her underwear down her legs and steps out of them.

She gets into the shower and I follow, closing the door behind us. She maneuvers so that my back is against the water as she grabs the soap from the shelf behind her. She lathers it up between her hands before putting it back. Her small, delicate hands start at my neck moving over the muscle and skin, massaging with the slippery liquid. The heat from the water and the steam rise in the shower, but all I can concentrate on is the feel of her wet slippery hands moving over my chest. I close my eyes and a moan leaves my lips as I feel her hand caress my small nipple.

She stops touching and I open my eyes to see her lathering more soap. I know where I want her to touch next, but she doesn't.

"Turn around Dragon, so I can wash your back."

I want to refuse, but figure as long as she's touching me I'm good, so I turn around and brace myself on the wall.

I groan feeling her hands move over my back and shoulders. She slowly moves lower and lower until her small hands are cupping my ass and massaging. I'm so distracted by the way her hand is kneading the muscle of my ass, I gasp in surprise as I feel the bar of soap slide between my cheeks.

I've never been one to have my ass played with, I've heard and seen how some of the brothers like that shit, but it's not for me. I'm about to tell her that when I feel her small finger push into me. This makes twice she's done that and fuck it feels good.

My head goes down at that moment because at that same time I feel her other tiny hand reach between my legs and massage my balls gently.

"Nicole," I groan, my eyes closing.

"Shhh… Dragon, I'm just playing." Her lips kiss my shoulder blade gently and then further down my back. She rolls my balls gently in her hand while she continues kissing me.

"Nicole… Mama…" I moan as she continues to tease me.

"I love your body, Dragon. I love every inch of you," she says as she bites my ass cheek, with just enough pressure that my dick trembles.

He's mine.

Those words echo in my mind again. Fuck.

"That's it, Mama, I can't take anymore," I growl in a voice even I don't recognize. I turn facing her, intent on sinking inside of her and fucking her hard.

I don't get that chance though because once I turn around it hits me. She is on her knees. I'm looking down at her and her tongue darts out and licks the head of my cock. I lean against the wall as I look at this woman, who owns me.

Her hair is darker when wet and it's plastered against her chest. It brushes the tops of her upturned nipples. Maybe it's the way the light is shining, maybe it's her or maybe it's just the effect of the alcohol still in my system, but the water looks like drops of shiny metal sliding over her skin.

"Nicole baby…" I groan. I can't finish because she takes my cock into her mouth at the same time her hand gently palms my balls, teasing them. "Fuck…"

Nicole moans her appreciation and the sound vibrates against my cock, increasing the pleasure.

He's mine.

Again the words echo in my head as she swallows my dick, taking it to the root and totally catching me off guard. I groan out watching myself disappear into her gorgeous mouth. I brace myself on the shower walls as I watch. I come out of my haze enough to reach down and pull on her nipples, loving the way she cries out in delight even with her mouth stuffed full of me.

"You have to stop, Mama. I'm going to blow and when I do I want to be in that sweet snatch of yours."

She ignores me and picks up her pace, using her hand to work in tandem with her mouth. Fuck she wants it and I'm going to give it to her. I grab her head and start fucking her hard. I try to hold back, I don't want to hurt her, but she doesn't let me. She sinks her nails into my ass and moves her mouth up and down, aided only by my hands on her head guiding her. I try to keep from going too far, but she demands every inch, every fucking inch. Just as I'm about to explode I pull away from her mouth and use my hand to aim my cock at her. I shoot my cum all over her face, down her breasts and watch as her tongue comes out to lap at whatever she can reach. Nicole might be every fantasy I've ever had.

"Fuck Mama...I'm sorry..." Well shit I just lied, I'm not a bit sorry. It was hotter than hell seeing her covered in *me* and I know instantly I want to do that again. Still, I know women don't like that shit and I don't want to do anything to push her away from me.

"I'm not," she says standing up and bringing my hands to her chest. Together we rub my cum into her chest and her head tilts back under the water spray to rinse the rest off. She's a fucking goddess, and how I got lucky enough that she claimed me as hers in front of everyone, fuck I still can't figure that out.

I pull her to me and kiss her. I feel raw and cut open inside. Life has been fucked up for me from the beginning. It wasn't so long ago I was thinking about taking Lips on as my old lady. Now I find myself wrapped up in knots over this blue eyed, dark blonde spitfire. Not only that, she seems to want me and is proud to be mine. I don't fucking get it. She should have never let me have her. I'm not a fool and I know she is way out of my league. I should let her go. I know it, but fuck if I will. I'm keeping her.

"Penny for your thoughts," Nicole says, dragging my eyes back down to her.

"I'm thinking I haven't given my woman pleasure yet," I lie.

"I beg to differ. I enjoyed every minute of what just happened."

Fuck. My heart even skipped a fucking beat. How fucking pussy whipped is that? My gut goes tight. Oh shit yeah, I'm in way over my head here.

I turn Nicole around so that her back is to me and push her up against the wall of the shower. I nudge her legs apart to give me room to work. I caress her ass moving down slowly to tease her pussy. I push my fingers in to make sure she is ready for me. She is fucking trembling for me. Again I hear her voice in my head.

He's mine.

I lean down and whisper in her ear.

"You're mine, Nicole. Totally fucking mine." I slam balls deep inside of her.

Nicole

I lie here quietly, letting Dragon think I am still asleep. He's standing in front of the window, the moon is shining off his body and it makes him look other-worldly. He is perfection standing. A Greek God couldn't hold a candle to him. Yet, as beautiful as he is, as perfect as the package is, inside he's broken and scarred and I am starting to fear I will never be able to touch what matters most... his heart.

I watch him for a good ten minutes and he doesn't move. He's getting lost in his thoughts and I know that's not good. I'm pretty much in the dark, but I know some heavy shit went down. The girls at the party were talking about one of their own betraying them. I may not understand MC life, but I'm not stupid to the way it works either. I figure I know what Dragon had to face and I don't want to think about it. It might make me a hypocrite, but I don't really care.

"Dragon baby?" I whisper into the room. He turns, walks over to me and gets back under the cover. I smile as he pulls me to him.

"Sorry Mama, I didn't mean to wake you."

"I just missed you," I tell him truthfully. I hold him close, the chill of his body making me shiver before I settle into him, letting him take some of my body heat.

Dragon leans down and kisses the top of my head.

"So fucking sweet," he says. I smile and kiss along his collar bone.

"You okay sweetheart?" I ask, knowing the truth but not going there, unless he shares first.

"Just got a lot on my mind tonight."

"Do you want to talk about it?" I ask, hoping he would.

"Don't want my shit to touch you Mama."

"If we're going to try and make this work Dragon, that's not very realistic."

"Okay then, want to keep you out of it for at least a little longer," Dragon sighs.

"I'm not going anywhere," I said, kissing him again in the same spot.

"You might change your mind if you know what kind of blood is on my hands Nicole."

"Do you want me here?" I ask, deciding a different approach is needed.

"Nowhere else Mama," he says, hugging me a little tighter in reaction.

"Then, I'm here."

Dragon lets silence take us over. I am a little disappointed, but still I know it will take time for him to get used to sharing with me. I need to be patient. I've already seen small changes in him.

I let my hand trail down his stomach, my fingers following the line of his tattoo. It's of a wolf howling with his fangs eerily covered in blood, and the words 'Savages MC' at a diagonal written in the blood. Underneath that the words, *Live Free or Die Trying* are placed. I have seen that insignia all through the club. It is on the arms or backs of each of the members, yet on Dragon it is different. On all the others it looked frightening, almost menacing, but on Dragon it is sad and beautiful.

Our room is dark and quiet. The sounds from the party in the main room had died down long ago. I pull closer to Dragon, our legs interlocked, his arm holding me at his side, my head resting on his shoulder. I can't remember ever being as happy as I am right now. I don't know why, but here in this moment, after everything we had done tonight, I feel like I've found where I belong.

My lips press a kiss over Dragon's heart. He can act mean and tough and I even understand why, but he has another side to him. A side he lets me see, a side that makes me want to reach out and never let him go. I love him. I can't deny it anymore. I'm not ready to share that with him though, if he had been listening in the shower he might know now.

It hasn't been long, and some would say nowhere near the time needed to feel as deeply as I did. I don't care what they say and it doesn't matter to me. I know that I love Dragon. Time and caution be damned.

"What's your real name?" I whisper. If he isn't ready to share the club with me, then I need this part of him. I need to know I'm not totally invested by myself.

Dragon sighs, "Mama I don't want to get into this shit tonight."

"Please?" I ask. It is important. In my heart I know now Dragon was it for me. If we don't work out, there will never be another man who will get all of me like I am willing to give him.

"Some kids don't have white picket fences Nicole. Hell, they don't even have houses."

"I know that Dragon."

"Knowing it and living it are two different things, Mama."

"And you lived it?" I asked. I can feel my stomach twisting.

"Fuck Mama, I burned in hell with it."

I let my hand move to his other side and pull him closer to me. I want to absorb his words, let him know I am here with him.

"Dragon is my name," he says tiredly, his eyes closed.

"Who gave you that name?" I'm trying to give him a minute away from the memories I had tripped.

"My brothers in the Army, said they could feel the scorch of my anger on the battlefield."

Having seen Dragon upset and on other heated occasions, I could firmly and wholeheartedly agree with that, so I say nothing. I just place another kiss on his chest and wait.

"I liked it, it was an honest name given to me by men who had become my family. So that's who I am now. The person before Dragon doesn't even exist now."

"And who was that man?" I ask, not sure why at this point I'm pushing, just knowing I need to.

"The name the city gave me."

"The city?" I ask, confused.

"Damn it, Nicole!"

"It's okay, Dragon. You don't…"

"Found in a dumpster, Mama, wrapped in a garbage bag. Just another whore's throw away, addicted to crack. Is that what you wanted to hear, Nicole? Are you proud you let that filth touch you?" Dragon growls out.

He sits up, on the side of the bed, his back to me. I sit behind and press against him, kissing the back of his neck and hugging him as tight as I could with my arms.

"I've never been prouder. I've never belonged to anyone in my life before you Dragon. I'm yours no matter what," I whisper into his ear, hoping the message gets through to him.

My heart is pounding. I knew Dragon's story was bad, but I didn't expect this. I feel like I am breaking in half, just picturing the story he painted. Someone threw out this magnificent man with the garbage. What a beautiful baby he must have been. He deserved to be loved, to be held and rocked to sleep. To be kissed and whispered to.

A tear falls from my eyes and I am glad he couldn't see it. Dragon wouldn't want pity from me. I can't show him that.

"That's who I am, Nicole. I survived and the doctors got the shit out of my system. I survived. End of the fucking story."

I had a feeling that was just the beginning of a horrible story. I am almost afraid to go further. Still, the fact it happened to this man, the fact that it happened to the man who owned my heart, made it imperative that I learn more. I want to heal him. I want to show him love and all the things he has never had in life. From this moment on, it was going to be my mission in life. Dragon would wake every morning, knowing someone loved him above all others.

I kiss the side of his neck and just hold him. I let the salty sweet of his skin soothe me. Maybe I shouldn't have pushed him, reliving this was hard on him and I knew beyond a shadow of a doubt, he didn't share this with anyone. I would let it drop for now. We had time, and eventually Dragon would know I am always here for him. I was about to distract him from the thoughts I had triggered when he surprised me.

"Lady at the first foster home agreed to take in the crack baby. I was a check, but for taking me off the hospital's hands, she got to name me."

Somehow I knew this wasn't going to be good, so I just

kissed the side of his neck again and waited.

"She thought it was fucking funny to name me something to remind me of what I was. I was born in West Detroit Mama. So the name I got on my papers was Detroit West. Fucking laugh riot, yeah?"

"I think it's a beautiful name."

Dragon pulls away from me, standing up. He stands in front of the window again. The moonlight shining through the room highlights his features and bounces off his dark skin. He is a work of art. His short cropped hair makes me want to run my fingers over it and feel the prickly texture that never fails to send instant tingles of heat through my body. The tone of his muscular legs, the width of his back and shoulders, the ink that decorated him and finally the freaking fabulous ass that jutted out in a way a woman just wanted to dig her nails into it and mark it as hers, all of it is perfection to me.

He stares outside, lost in thought. I don't know what to say to break the mood he is in. It's my fault, I shouldn't have pushed him. He turns around quickly and his eyes lock on me. I could feel them searing me. That, right there, was the look of the dragon.

"Don't kid yourself, Mama. There is not a damn thing beautiful about me."

"You are to me," I insisted, giving up and lying back down. I can't prove it to him, not now. Maybe he'll see in time, that to me he is.

It wasn't the perfection on the outside that made him that way either. It was the scarred broken parts inside of him that he overcame every day. He could say he was no good, but he had been better to me than any one person in my life. He made me feel like I mattered, and with the exception of Dani, I don't think anyone ever had. I am totally and irrevocably in love with Detroit 'Dragon' West.

A look comes across his face that I don't understand, it is anger almost. He stalks over to the bed and grabs my legs, pulling me towards the end of the bed and spreading my body open to him.

"Don't fucking romanticize me Nicole. Don't you even fucking try it, that won't hold water," he growled. "I'm the filthy bastard you stupidly let between your legs and I'm not giving it up until I'm ready."

He grabs his cock and rubs it back and forth against my clit, giving me pressure but definitely not enough. I'm still wet from earlier and the look of him between my legs holding his thick, hard cock, combined with the way he is watching my body open and beg for him? I might just explode instantly.

"Look at your fucking pussy, begging for me. Is this what you want Nicole? You want to take a walk on the wild side and let the monster fuck you till you get bored and move back to your fucking house on the hill?" Dragon growls, and then pushes inside of me.

I watch him, my eyes never leaving his as he begins teasing my clit with his hand and moving in and out of me at a slow, intense pace.

"I'll never get enough, Dragon."

"Shut the fuck up and feel me inside of you," he growls, watching every time he slams inside of me. My body rocks with each plunge he makes, my breasts bounce and I inch up further on the mattress with the force of his thrusts.

"I'll always want you, Dragon."

I moan and he grunts, but says nothing in response.

"I love you!" I call out as I feel myself going over the edge.

Dragon's eyes immediately hit mine. I look into them as my orgasm takes over.

"I love you Dragon. I love you," I whisper again on a low emotion filled moan.

His orgasm overtakes him in that moment. I feel him shooting inside of me and I tighten myself on his body as much as I can.

Dragon leans down and kisses me hard, his tongue owning my mouth and exploring every inch he could find, while his body shudders in release.

I let my tongue dance with his as tears leak out of the sides of my eyes. I didn't plan on telling him, but he had bombarded me with so many things I needed to let him know how I really felt. Now I was the one left feeling raw and exposed, but instead of worrying about that, I decide to concentrate on our connection.

Dragon pulls my body closer and angles us back on the pillows. Dragon is lying partly on me and partly on the bed. My left leg is thrown over his hip and I've dug the heel of my foot into his ass. He tries to pull out of me and I moan my protest and exert pressure with my leg and the arm I have wrapped around him. It makes him stop and I kiss his chest in appreciation.

"Baby..." he started and his voice was gruff. I hope that means that my declaration has at least broken through a little.

"Don't want you to leave me, please? Stay inside of me, however long you can, please Dragon? I want you in me," I whisper, kissing his chest again.

Dragon groans and adjusts us so I am lying on top of him now.

"Okay, Mama." He says kissing the top of my head, "Whatever you want."

"You, I want you," I whisper, and the last thing I remember as I fell asleep is Dragon placing another kiss on the top of my head with three words I never want to forget.

"You got me."

Chapter 9

Nicole

It's raining. The rain makes me miss him more. I hear it falling as I slide my hand down my body. My skin is soft. There's a slight chill to it and I can feel the goose bumps rise behind my touch as I follow the path around my breasts. I have never liked my breasts, always hated that they were too big, not as perky and round like the pictures I've seen or even Danielle's. She's got gorgeous breasts. I've always been jealous of them, but not since I've been with Dragon. He makes me love my body and makes me crave how it felt when he took my breasts in his large callused hands. How it felt when he placed his lips on my nipple and slowly moved his tongue around and sucked it into his mouth. How it felt to feel him sucking and biting. God I love his bite.

Last night was wonderful, beyond wonderful really. I fell asleep with Dragon inside of me and woke up hours later with him taking me again. He was insatiable. I never knew men like him even existed outside of books or movies. I stretch and my body feels sore and well used. I could almost purr like a contented cat.

Even better, I smell of him this morning. I can smell his sex on me. Hours later and I can still feel him leaking from between my legs and I should hate it, but I don't. I freaking revel in the knowledge that I belong to Dragon 'Detroit' West. I revel in the fact that last night he gave me a piece of him very few people get, if any.

I think back over the night we shared. The revelations that were made, the discussions, the sex that was down and dirty and so freaking hot, we probably would have spontaneously combusted if I hadn't fallen asleep on him. My Dragon was a dirty, dirty man and he made me the same. I think I like being a dirty girl. I feel freer with him than I had ever felt in my life.

I close my eyes and listen to the rain, wishing Dragon was still here. He woke me around five this morning, telling me he had some club business to see to, but he would be back. The fact he even bothered to wake me up to tell me goodbye, I was sure signaled some kind of change in our relationship. I just wasn't sure of what kind.

I am lying here thinking about everything I had discovered about Dragon when my phone vibrates on the nightstand. I reach over to get it and check the message.

Hey can I tear u away from Dragon today?

Yep, she's still pissed.

Dragon's gone. What's up?

I'm in a situation. Meet me at the house in an hour?

Will do.

Well that was vague, and worrisome. Dani never asks for help, especially when she was somewhat pissed at you. I get up from the bed with a sigh. First order of business was a shower and food. Then hopefully I could see to Dani before Dragon realizes I'm gone. He expected me to stay here at the club while on lockdown. Normally, I wouldn't test him, but Dani is my girl and I didn't like this friction between us. Dragon would just have to understand.

After a quick shower, quick because staying in there and

remembering the night before with Dragon was defeating the reason for the shower, I walk through the club into the back room which also happens to be the kitchen. Irish was in there with a prospect I had met earlier. They called him Nailer. He was African American like Dragon, but that was where the similarities ended. He was just as broad and built but his skin was lighter and he looked softer than Dragon somehow. I figured his nickname was pretty much horn dog material, but hadn't bothered to ask.

"Hey boys," I say, trying not to take offense because they stopped talking immediately when I came into the room. I know Dragon said club business was club business, but really.

"Hey Nic. What ya' into today?" Irish asks, handing me an empty plate.

I went about filling it with some scrambled eggs and sausage that had been set out in dishes along the bar, added a piece of toast and sat down across from them.

"Got some stuff going on with Dani later, that's about it. Hey Irish? What days am I working this week? I haven't seen the new schedule," I asked him, putting some butter on my toast.

"Uh Nic, Dragon said you weren't working at the club anymore."

I stopped putting my butter on halfway through and looked up at Irish.

"He what?" I growled.

"Hey take it up with the Boss. All I know is what he told me and he says under no circumstances is his woman schlepping drinks to a bunch of drunk, horny bastards."

I finished buttering my toast. I was kind of pissed, but I couldn't help snorting at the way Irish said it. Plus, Dragon had apparently called me his woman. There was no way I could be mad after that. I took a bite of the toast and vowed to plan my attack with Dragon later.

"What time will Dragon and the men be back?" I ask, pushing my eggs around my plate.

"Probably late girl. Crush and him went to the prison to see Dancer and then had some other things to do."

I nodded, finishing up my toast and deciding my eyes were bigger than my stomach.

"Okay boys I'm out of here I need to go check on my girl and pack up some more clothes."

"I thought Dragon wanted you to stay here because of the lock down?" Nailer asked.

"He wouldn't want you to just leave Nic. Nailer is right," Irish added.

"I'm just going to the house. That's what, a twenty minute drive at the most? I have to get some more clothes and shit and Dani called. I shouldn't be gone long."

"Take Nailer with you. I'd go myself but the bar is expecting a delivery soon," Irish said.

I looked at Nailer with a shake of my head.

"I'll probably bore you silly, so if you don't want to go…"

"I'm ready when you are."

"Whatever then, let's hit the road. See ya later Irish."

"Later, Nic."

* * *

"Okay, Nailer. I've seen Dragon mad, so I know how he got his name. Irish is pretty self-explanatory and even Crusher or

Bull. Should I just assume Nailer means you are a horn dog?" I ask from the passenger seat of the club's SUV. Nailer insisted we take this black Chevy Tahoe, as opposed to my Mercedes. He mumbled something about his Tahoe being manlier. Men are so silly!

"Well I'm a man and I think we're all pretty much pussy chasers."

"Well... some chase dicks," I said philosophically.

"Okay, well I don't though, but even so, I used to work construction, so hence the nickname."

"Well dang Nailer, that's kind of a boring story," I said with a grin.

"Would it help if I told you Bull got his name because he was hung like one?" He joked turning into the driveway of the house Dani and I had rented.

"I don't think I'm supposed to know that kind of information about Bull. Oh my God, I'll never be able to look at the man again now."

Nailer laughed and we got out of the SUV. I had been dreading being in a car with someone I didn't know, but Nailer made me laugh. So far I had to say, with the exception of the bitch that I had to put in her place, I liked all of Dragon's "family".

Dani's car was in the driveway, so at least I wouldn't have to wait around until she got home.

I opened the door and walked in still laughing with Nailer and because of that, was completely unprepared for what happened next.

The smallest guy Dani left with the other night came out from behind the door and used the butt of his gun to hit Nailer in the head. Nailer went down with a horrible thud. I screamed and immediately the man wraps his beefy looking hand around my mouth and drags me further inside.

I try biting him, but he holds my head so tight, I can't move enough to get away from him. I know there is fear in my eyes, you couldn't really help it in this situation, but I'm still pissed as hell at myself for allowing it. I look over at Dani and she doesn't appear alarmed. There's something in her eyes, I wasn't sure what it was exactly, but she starts walking towards me.

"Calm down Nic. It's not what you think. Tiny and me are trying to save you. Girl, you just don't know what that man you are with has done."

I elbow the idiot holding me and Dani nods at him and he lets me go.

"Are you crazy?" I immediately go down on the floor to check on Nailer. He's breathing, but definitely out cold with a knot the size of Texas on the back of his head.

"Nic, I had to get you away from that club. You don't know what they're doing!" Dani said, reaching down to pull me away. I stubbornly refused to let her.

"Have you lost your freaking mind?"

"Nic!"

"Dani! How the fuck do you know anything is going on? You spent what? A couple nights with this asshole and decide everything he's telling you is the fucking truth?"

"He had pictures Nic. You should see what Dragon did to his own man! Here look at them! You can't stay with him Nic, he'll hurt you!"

I hear the panic in her voice, so I try to count to ten and calm my temper. Then I take the camera she's pushing at me. I click the review button on the back and scan through the photos captured on the little screen.

Okay my stomach knots up at what I see. Dragon is torturing some man lying in a …bathtub? The man is badly beaten. There's one picture where it appears that Dragon was cutting off his fingers maybe? It's hard to tell and the picture is obviously taken through a window and at a good distance away.

"Why do you have these pictures?" I ask Dani, and the man I remember Skull called Tiny the other night. He has a smug ass look on his face. I don't like him. That thought rings clear over a myriad of emotions hammering through me at the moment. Dani looks at me like I have three heads.

"That's all you have to say? Did you see what he was doing to that poor man?"

Good question, I guess. I mean I did see it, but I had also seen pictures at the club of the girl that had been beaten. I knew this was the club business Dragon had been handling. If this man had been the one who had done that to the girl, and if he had also been one of Dragon's men like Dani insinuated, it didn't excuse him, but it sure as hell put a different light on the situation.

"I'm not discussing Dragon's business with you Dani, I'm asking why the fuck these pictures were taken in the first place?"

"Tiny is in charge of following Dragon and his crew when they are in Skull's city to make sure they don't do shit LIKE THIS! Nic, you can't be so far gone over Dragon that you can't see how wrong this is? Jesus."

I act like I'm going through the pictures, but instead eject the memory card out the side and slide it into my pants pocket. Maybe I am a fool, but I believe in him and I'm not about to leave anything that might be used against him.

"Get the fuck out of my house," I yell when I finish, turning the camera off and tossing it across the room.

"Not going to happen bitch," Tiny smugly says. It's then I notice the look on his face. Yeah, thinking I just don't like him was understating shit—like a lot.

"What do you want from me?" I ask with a disgusted snarl, trying to figure out how in the hell to get out of this mess.

"To play with you sweet cheeks, maybe I'll do you and your girl at the same time. Dani here likes to party. The more the merrier, right baby?"

God he makes my stomach turn. I watch Dani's face as it goes white. Dani has some amazing qualities, but when it comes to men, she's worse than me. The thought of letting this man anywhere near me makes me gag.

"You touch me and Dragon will feed you your dick and balls on a silver platter."

"Think you're overestimating your appeal *puta*. Dragon's known for liking lots of pussy, you're just the flavor of the day. You're not my type so much, but I'll fuck your ass while you're eating out your girl. Now enough of this shit. Strip before I decide your fat ass is more trouble than it's worth."

"Tiny baby stop it, you're going to scare Nic. Besides, I told you I don't party with other women," Dani said. I could tell she was trying to distract him so I could get away, the panicked look in her eyes when she shot me a pleading glance told me so. I couldn't leave her and Nailer here alone though. I move my body so I'm blocking Nailer's torso, then use my hand to see if he had any kind of weapon on him I could use.

I might have thrown up in my mouth a little when Dani actually kisses the creep. Ugh, I would have to gargle twenty times a day for the rest of my life.

Still when she hikes her leg up on his hip and starts taking his shirt off, I figure I might have a shot of getting us out of this fucked up mess, if Nailer just had something I could use.

Eureka! A knife, though I would have much rather had a gun. Dragon should really talk to his men about carrying weapons at all times. I mean seriously, what kind of bad ass protector didn't have a freaking gun??

I palm the knife and hide it behind my back. I'm trying to come up with a plan as I watch Dani practically mouth raping Tiny. Ugh, I'm suddenly glad I didn't eat anything more than toast.

The only thing I can come up with kind of sucks. Stab yuck man, preferably in the balls for his comment about doing me and Dani, then running with my girl and getting the heck out of Dodge. The problem with this sucky ass plan was that it left Nailer unprotected. I hated it, but I figured he'd be running after me and Dani. Actually, I was hoping I'd leave him in bad enough shape he couldn't do anything again. Yeah, it was a sucky ass plan for sure.

Tiny pushes Dani away finally, but I could tell from the look in his eyes it was only so I could join in. I don't know where Bad Nicole had gone lately, but if she was here, I'd totally let her take over and stab this bastard between the eyes.

"Come on over here *puta*. Let me see what you got."

I push the knife down the back of my pants hanging the handle on the rim of my jeans. I send up a silent prayer I don't cut myself or the knife doesn't fall and cut my sixty dollar lingerie set I'm wearing. My luck it will and then fall to the floor where it leaves me, fucked, and sadly that's also in the literal sense.

Ewww, don't want him after having Dragon.

Well hell there's Bad Nicole now, but why did she sound so panicked and afraid?

Oh yeah because fuck, I am. I walk over a few steps shooting Dani a *I'm going to kill you later look.* I almost feel guilty when I see the tears in her eyes. Dani is a beautiful person, but she doesn't really think before she leaps. Me? I normally over think, but I'm not seeing that as a negative at the moment.

"Take off your shirt. I want to see the merchandise."

God I don't want to, but I need him to think I'm going to go along with this plan until I get close enough to do some damage.

Please God, let me do some damage.

I paste on what I hope is a scared little girl face. Shit there is not a lot of acting required, I'm pretty damn scared. I lift my pink camouflage thermal shirt off and over my head throwing it on the floor. I loved that shirt and it was uber warm, but I vow that if I survive this, I'm never wearing that damn shirt again.

"Oh yeah look at those luscious tits. I'm definitely going to bury my cock in those fuckers. I think you're starting to grow on me *puta*."

I want to kill him.

"I've never done anything like this..."

Fuck. Fuck. Fuck.

"That's okay *puta*, lucky for you I have."

I get closer to him and I feel Dani step back. I'm trying to shore up my courage and keep my hands from shaking. I'm only going to get one shot at this.

"Should I...take my bra off?" I ask and thank the lucky stars above I wore a bra that clasps in the back today.

"Oh yeah, show ole' Tiny what you got for him."

He asked right? Deep breath…one…two…My hand goes back as if to unhook my bra, but instead I move it down to grasp the knife. Three…. I tighten my hand up around the knife, praying it was as big and sharp as it seemed and in my panic I think of three places to stab. Balls are way too low and would take too long and I could miss. Eye, I could hit it but he might have time to block it and he is sure to be a lot stronger than me. So I go for the gut. It's closer, I can reach it easier and he has less time to fight off the attack.

I scream as I stab him. I'm not sure it helps but it makes me feel better. The knife slices in and it takes some force, but I manage to get it in deep. Blood spews forth and the sight of it going around my hand and out of the wound is horrible. I want to hold onto the knife, but my hand is so slick I can't. As the bastard falls back against the couch, cussing and calling me names that would make a sailor blush, I yell at Dani to run. We take off with him cursing in the background. I don't look back. I read somewhere that looking back is wrong, bad wrong. Besides that, in all of the scary movies, the silly bitches that look back always get their throats slashed. We run towards the SUV that Nailer and I rode in. Fuck no fucking keys!

"Tiny has mine!" Dani yells out panicking big time now, but I'm right there with her.

"We have to hit the hills. We'll circle around and come back out on the main road by Dragon's compound!"

"Nic! You know what the hills are like, it's impossible to follow a back road!"

"Just do it Dani! Jesus, we don't have time to debate it."

We take off running towards the hills and I just pray we can get away and to safety before Tiny finds us. While we're running towards the hills, I hear the front screen door open and I know that's not good.

Shit.

Chapter 20

Nicole

Okay, in hindsight, my plan to hit the hills wasn't a very good one. Dani and I had been on the run now for a good hour and I wasn't sure how long it would take a person to walk fifteen miles but I was pretty sure we had done it. We're currently sitting on a log right now trying to catch our breath.

When we first started, I thought I heard Tiny chasing after us, but it has been silent since. I'm hoping the fucker had died from his stab wound, but I'm not holding my breath. It seems my luck is not that great.

I'm freezing. Dani hadn't been wearing a jacket and while she offered me her shirt, I figured I had more meat on my bones and could withstand the cold longer. I'm starting to think that was a fucked up idea. I'm so cold and tired at this point that I'm numb.

"Shit Nic, I'm sorry. It's just Dragon went so crazy the other night with Skull and then I saw those photos. I was worried about you! You have to understand…"

Dani had been crying and I totally understood what she was saying, but I couldn't lie and say I wasn't pissed too.

"It's okay Dani, let's just concentrate on getting out of this mess," I say, getting up to continue walking, leaving her to follow me.

"You're still pissed," she says, as we start trudging through the briars and trees.

"You shouldn't have tried to set me up. You didn't even know that man! You put both of us in danger without even thinking!"

"He hasn't been like that before today, I swear Nic."

"Oh wow, so he was like great for a whole freaking day or two and just turned psycho, nutty, crazy the last fucking hour?" I bite back. Okay, I might be a little madder than I first estimated.

"That's not fair! You haven't known Dragon that long either, and it's clear he's a little unhinged. Did you not see those photos?"

"I did, but what I know that you don't Dani, is that Dragon is good to me and he's a good man. There are things going on at his club. I don't understand it and we haven't talked about it, but I know there was a woman raped and beaten and she's in bad shape. I trust Dragon enough to believe that whatever he did, there was a reason!"

"It still doesn't make it right!" Dani argued.

"I heard the boys talking Dani. The victim was a sweet and innocent woman that they all thought a lot of. She was beaten unconscious and raped! I don't care what you think is right. If that had been you, I would have wanted Dragon to get revenge too!"

"You're freaking whacked. You're so wrapped up in Dragon you can't see he's not a good guy! You do not need to be mixed up in this shit Nic."

"What is your problem?" I yell and turn on her. Another mistake! I should be letting her ass lead so she'd hit the briars first. She at least has a long sleeved shirt on!

"I'll tell you what my problem is! You were supposed to sleep with him and have some fun! Not just agree to move into

174

his clubhouse and become his personal bitch! You have no idea what you're getting into with a man like him!"

It hits me then what is really wrong with Dani. I should have guessed it earlier but it just didn't click into place. I take a deep breath.

"Dani, Dragon isn't Michael."

"Michael didn't seem like Michael in the beginning Nic. Even *you* have to admit that. Hell, you liked him!"

"I did and you're right. I know Michael fucked you up in a big way. I get that Dani, but you're reacting in all the wrong ways here. You have got to quit letting the past control your future. Michael is gone."

"Some scars don't heal," she grumbles and pushes past me.

I sigh. There wasn't much more I could say. Dani had every right to feel like she did.

"Dani, Dragon protects me. He'd never hurt me."

"Save it Nic. I saw the look in his eyes. I'm all too familiar with that look and with the excuses women make."

I let it go. It didn't matter what I told her about Dragon, she wasn't going to listen. Besides, I had bigger worries.

"Hold up, I know we've passed that damn rock before," I observe, turning around to stare at the huge boulder that looks like one we would have used as a big slide growing up.

"Fuck!" Dani growls and that about summed it up. "I told you going into the hills was a bad idea! Son of a bitch!"

Now I can clearly realize that Dani didn't deal well with panic. Good to know, wish I had known that earlier!

"Calm down. We'll just turn right and start going that way to head towards the road. Surely we can get our bearings then," I rationalize.

"I thought you said the road was too dangerous!"

"For God's sake, you're not listening to me about anything else, why listen now?" I huff and push in front of her. I start walking to the right. She could follow or not at this point.

Chapter 21

Dancer

"I told you I don't want you here."

It was hateful of me to say that and I knew it. I looked over at my brothers Dragon and Crusher, the two men who had been my only family since I was fifteen. We grew up in hell together. We knew more about each other than any one person should ever know about the other. I'd die for each of the men sitting in front of me. I would eat a motherfucking bullet for them and not blink an eye. Still, I didn't want them here. I looked around the cold little 12x12 room that was barren and devoid of color. That's how it's meant to be though, because from the day that door slammed behind me, there has been no color. Five hundred and sixty four days in this place and every day grew darker. Thirteen thousand, five hundred and thirty six hours...I glance at the clock high up on the wall... and twenty odd minutes, since my life became this hell.

The silver of the table matches the cold silver clasped around my wrists. The fucking guards keep these on me all the time lately. It's just another way of poking the bear, another way to mock and belittle and get to me. I don't let that shit show, but I know it's working. Deep down inside, I feel another layer of respect torn away and I fought hard to get that shit. It took years to make a life I was fucking proud of and I did it. It took one act to destroy it and hell, the fucked up truth of it all was I'd do it again. Maybe I really was the moron the guards liked to call me.

"You knew we'd be here just like always," Crusher says, looking his normal cocky self. I was like that once, wasn't I? I thought nothing could touch me too. I was wrong, so fucking wrong.

"How ya' doin' brother?" Dragon asks.

My eyes move over to him. He wasn't a pretty mother fucker that was for sure. Big, dark, scarred and hard as nails, that was Dragon. He looked a little different today though. Dragon was a self-contained time bomb, wrapped so fucking tight that the brothers and I would take bets on what would happen when he finally blew. The Dragon before me now looked relaxed and at ease.

"Fucking laugh a minute here Drag. Since you fuckers made the trek here, maybe you can tell me why?"

"Been hearing shit and I can't help but wonder why you haven't reached out to us Dancer."

"Not a fucking thing you can do Drag, some things are out of your hands."

"Not fucking likely Dancer and don't pull this shit again," Dragon responds.

I know he thinks he can help, but he has no idea the fucked up shit that goes on behind these doors. I can't allow myself to get my hopes up that anything my boy does will change things. Chances are, if he does anything it will just make things worse. A fuck of a lot worse.

"Let it go Drag. I know you want to help, but some things you can't do and chances are you'll end up making it worse."

"Dancer man…" Dragon growled, raking his hand over his hair in frustration. I knew this was killing him. If he really knew what was going on with me…fuck. I can't think about that anyway, because no one will ever know what happened here. If I ever see the light of day, I plan on drinking it out of my memory.

"What's up with you anyway? You seem different?" I ask, mostly to change the subject but also because part of me wanted to know what the fuck was up.

Crush laughs his cocky little snort of a laugh and I watch as Dragon smiles. He fucking smiled. What the hell? I'd known Dragon more years than I could count and I can't ever remember the son of a bitch smiling.

"Bossman has a woman," Crush answers, stretched out and grinning like a damn Cheshire cat towards Dragon.

"Fuck off," Dragon says shaking his head.

"Dragon always has women," I reply and it was the truth. Women flocked to the bastard.

"Not like this one Dancer, man. This one is special. She has all his shit tied up."

Dragon didn't even argue. Holy hell!

"You'll meet her soon Dancer. Eagle is working on getting your appeal decision handled this week."

Eagle was the club lawyer and sharp as a fucking tack. If anyone could get it done, it would be him. You would think after all this time hope would have died a bloody, fucking violent death. Apparently it hasn't, because I can feel the quickening of my heartbeat. I want to tell him not to worry about it but I can't make the lie come. I want out of here. Fuck, if I don't get out of here soon, I may do like that poor schmuck in cellblock C last night and twist my neck to escape. I don't know what is waiting for me in the next world, but the way I figure it, even hell can't get worse than this place.

"Visit is over girls, time to leave. Jacob here has a date with the little girl's room. I got a sparkling new tooth brush for him."

Fucking prick! I get out of here he's the first one I'm killing. The very fucking first and I'm going to make it hurt. They think I was a killer before I came in here? They have no idea what the fuck they have turned me into.

"Later boys," I say, as Dixon pulls me up and pushes me back towards my hell.

"Head up brother, it's coming, you got my word."

I turn to look at Dragon. Could he see the bleakness in my eyes? Could he read the crap that had happened to me since I've been behind bars?

I just nod and turn away. As I walk back into hell, I do my best to beat down the hope that tries its damnedest to take root in my chest.

Dragon

"Fuck man there's more going on than even our informant is telling us," Crush says as we walk out the door. I try not to wince at the clanging of the doors, but I do just the same.

"I know." We walk towards the visitor's area where the lockers we were given to hold our personal items are located.

"So what the fuck are we going to do? We need to get him out of this hell hole."

"Call Eagle, tell him to speed this shit up. I don't care what money is involved or who we need to pay."

Crush didn't respond, but there was nothing much to say. We waited while the guard behind the counter took our claim ticket. He pushed cell phones and billfolds across to us. We grab them and leave. I hated that I was so relieved to get out of there, leaving my brother in there to rot. Hell yeah, Eagle needed to get on the ball.

Once we made it outside I put my shades back on and stop when I get on my bike. Shit, maybe I am pussy whipped, but all I know is I want to check in with my woman. That's when I notice I have twenty missed calls from Irish and Nailer. Crusher got on his bike beside me, but he didn't talk. Maybe he could tell from my face shit was up.

"Yo, what the fuck is going on?" I say as soon as Irish picks up the phone.

"Dragon, man Nicole is missing."

Holy fuck, my heart hurts. With three words I knew more fear than I had ever felt in my life.

"Motherfucker, I left her in your care! You better be fucking joking and let me say right now that fucking shit ain't funny and I'm going to personally pull your head out of your ass backwards…"

"Dragon, her girl called and asked her to meet at their house. I made her take Nailer. Hell Dragon, Nailer said it was an ambush. He opened the door and some fucker knocked him out cold. When he woke up your woman and her girl and whoever the hell hit him were gone but…. Shit man."

"What damn it?" I felt a knot in my chest and fear, total fear. What the hell was wrong with me?

"Fuck man… there was blood everywhere."

I think my heart stopped. Whatever I felt in that moment went beyond fear.

"What about the cameras at the house?" I said trying to think. Anything the club owned had cameras on them but fuck, the cameras on that old house were ancient. Why the hell hadn't I thought to change them sooner?"

"It looks like the girls got away into the hills. Some fucker came out behind them, got in a car and left."

"So, he didn't follow them?" I asked trying to catch my breath.

"No, but we haven't heard from Nic. The boys have been combing the hills and the main road."

"Crush and I are about an hour out. Call the Ohio Chapter and tell them we won't be there today. Then you put every fucking man we have out searching and you find her. If she's hurt I'm taking it out on your motherfucking ass for letting her leave during lockdown!"

I look at Crusher while I start up my bike.

"Home, now!" I order, not explaining the rest. I figure he heard enough of the conversation I didn't need to clue him in. My fucking palms are sweaty and my heart is beating out of my chest. I'm not a praying man. I figure God turned his back on me before I was born. It's the only explanation for the way my life started, but right now though, I find myself praying and praying hard.

I need this woman. Last night cemented that for me, when she held me and told me she just wanted me. Fuck. No one had ever ripped me open like that before. They sure hadn't claimed me and been proud of that shit. In my experience women wanted to fuck the Prez because I was the Prez, but that was about it. Nicole could care less about the club or my position in it. I still didn't understand what it was between us, but after last night I know this girl is it for me. I have to have her. I have to keep her and fuck, she has to be safe. She just has to be.

Hold on Mama, I'm coming.

I repeat that mantra in my head over and over, praying she can somehow hear me.

Nicole

Okay, it sucks but I'm ready to admit it. I have no fucking idea where we are. I thought we were heading towards the road, I really did, but we've been walking forever now and there's no sign of a fucking road. In fact, the hill seems to be going up instead of down. Shouldn't it go down if I'm getting close to the road? I fall back against a tree and Dani does something similar across from me. We don't talk. Neither one of us are happy with each other at this point. We're cold, we're tired, and we're scared. I refuse to list scared first, though truly the fear I feel inside is like this giant knot threatening to choke me at this point. Worse I'm horribly numb. The radio had said the high today would be forty but it feels like fifteen. I'm so frozen I don't think I'll ever get warm again. I close my eyes and picture Dragon. He probably doesn't even know I'm missing. He was going to be gone all day. Dani and I had both been trying to use our cell phones but no signal. That's the thing about living in the Appalachian Mountains, cell service sucked donkey balls. I would almost suck donkey balls to get out of this mess. Shit no, I'd make Dani do it. Bitch owed me, even if she didn't admit it, and surely that couldn't be as bad as sleeping with that creep I had stabbed.

Oh my God, I stabbed someone. I should feel remorse I guess. The last hour or two or however long we'd been out here, I was mostly wishing I had been able to Lorena Bobbit his ass, or dick as it were.

"We need to keep moving," Dani said.

I wanted to ignore her because I figured she deserved that shit.

"Feel free, I need to take a minute to breathe," I grumble instead. I sounded like a spoiled two year old but I didn't care. I blame Dani, even if I understand her reasons behind it. I love my girl but she got us in this mess and I want to slap the shit out of her.

"I'm sorry Nic." She sounded so miserable, I felt a little guilty.

"Forget it. I understand, but you've got to trust me when I tell you Dragon is nothing like Michael."

Dani didn't say anything. I could tell from her face she didn't believe me, but she was wise enough to let it go, so I did too. She'd see in time, because despite what Dani said, despite the photos, despite everything, if I managed to survive this, I was totally going back to Dragon. I plan on holding him tight and never letting go.

"Should we try getting off the trail and sliding down the mountain to see if it might end up near the road?" Dani asked, and I could hear the fear in her voice. This was because when she said slide, she meant it. I had looked over the edge a time or two and it was more a cliff that was steep enough, falling off would most likely kill either of us. The mountains were gorgeous to look at, but clearly I should have listened closer to all those news reports about lost or injured hikers.

"Hell if I know at this point Dani. You know my parents trips to Lexington and Louisville were their idea of recreation. I know shit about climbing hills or directions apparently."

"Did you hear that?" she asks.

My body stiffens because I did. It sounded like branches snapping. Someone's coming. We stare at each other in panic and then Dani nudges with her head and points to a big rock behind her. It's not much but we make our way to it as quiet as we can to hide. Once we crouch down behind it, we sit and wait. When she grabs my hand, I hold on as tight as my numb fingers will let me.

"Alright bitch it's time for you two to come out. I know you're here but Irish tells me I don't have time to watch you squirm anymore. It's time we finish the game."

I would have thought he was bluffing if I hadn't heard a gun cocked on my right side. It sounds so chillingly loud even over the man's yelling.

I look over to see one of the last faces I expected. I almost feel relief but the other guy's words register in my numb brain.

"Irish?" I ask confused.

"Sorry Nic, just business. You got caught up in it. It's time Dragon is brought down and sadly girl, you are a sure way to keep him so wrapped up in his head he has no idea what's going on," he says, grabbing my arm and pulling me up. He lets me go, then grabs Dani by the hair of the head. He holds a gun to her as he urges us around the rock.

Another man is on the other side holding a gun. I don't know him. In fact I'm pretty sure I've never seen him before.

"How could you betray Dragon like this? He thinks of you as his brother?" I ask Irish. I'm not really trying to stall at this point. My mind is racing on how to get out of this, but really I'm pretty sure I'm going to die. I try to keep the tears from falling though, because I don't want to give them that victory.

"Just business, Nic. Dragon and Dancer pissed off the wrong people. The same people offered me a sweet deal to help them get revenge. Club makes a fuck of a lot of money, but Dragon's gone soft trying to keep everything legal. Once I'm in control and part of the Phoenix's pipeline, I can live in the Bahamas and rake in the cash."

"So you're betraying your brother for money?"

"Fucking shut it. What are you doing telling this whore our business?" the other man hollers out.

Because he's a moron!

Bad Nicole whispers and though that is a hundred percent certainty, I fear I know the real reason.

"What does it matter anyway? She'll be dead and we'll be long gone by the time Dragon finds her or her friend."

Oh yeah see, I totally knew the real reason.

"It matters. You don't follow instructions well! I know I told you to make sure Dragon didn't find out about this until the deed was done, yet here we are."

"I had to report in after Nailer came through, if I hadn't it would have been too suspicious. This way I can still play my role and spy on Dragon until you make your big move," Irish defends.

The other man looked totally unconvinced, but instead of responding asks, "Which one of you killed my friend Tiny?"

I should feel guilt that he died, but I can't seem to drum it up.

"That'd be me, but I thought he survived. You'll excuse me if I don't shed any tears over him," I say trying to sound badass. In truth I'm shaking inside and terrified. If I somehow survived this, I don't think I'll ever forget the way it feels to have a gun pointed at you.

"Oh he lived, but I had to kill him for being such a fucking moron," the man explains, as if he's talking about his grocery list.

"Well since you're doing the world a favor and ridding it of morons, maybe you could turn the gun on yourself," Dani piped up, and if I hadn't been so terrified I would have smiled.

The man looks at Dani and curls his lips and then just shoots her. I scream and go to her, falling down as I try to catch her. He shot her in the leg, and while that's a good place to get shot, if you had to get shot, there's instantly a lot of blood. I tear her shirt and try and stuff it on the wound, pushing it tight while the two men above us are laughing.

"A pity, Tiny spoke highly of you. I was going to add you to my stable. Can't stand a mouth like that though. Of course, if you survive I could cut your tongue out and still use you. Hmmm…" The pig seemed to truly be considering this.

"I'm going to meet up with the others. Take care of the whores and meet us at the docks."

"Might be more powerful if Nicole here is a gift," Irish suggests cryptically, and I don't know what this gift is, but I'm thinking it's not good.

"True, but think how much fun it'll be to deliver both. Just do your job and be quick about it."

"You got it."

With that, the other guy leaves out the way he came. Irish walks around in front of us and I want to kill him. He seems so calm, so detached while Dani lays there bleeding out. How could I have ever thought he was a good guy?

"Aw Nic girl, don't look at me like that. This is just

business. You just picked the wrong dick to hang onto. I was actually planning on giving you a go, but I'm sick of Dragon's leftovers. So you pretty much sealed your own fate."

"I wouldn't fuck you if you were the last man on earth."

"Don't make me prove you a liar girl. We both know I can. I'm tempted actually, but I don't have the time and unlike Dragon, I like to enjoy my women," he says walking closer to me.

He grabs my hair and pulls me away from Dani. She's not talking at all now since she looks like she passed out. At least I hope that is what happened. I feel the panic begin to overwhelm me. I try to strike out at him, hit him, claw him, do anything, but he takes the butt of his gun and slams it into the side of my face.

He must not have done it full strength because it doesn't knock me out, but I am literally seeing stars. I fall back to the ground looking up at Irish, or rather a couple of him. My vision is blurry and he swims in front of me. I register he's aiming his gun at me and I realize it's over. I'm half laying on Dani and she didn't even move, so I figure I've already lost her. I close my eyes and picture Dragon's face one more time. The way he looked before I fell asleep last night when he told me I had him. I don't know what comes after this world, but I pray whatever it is I'll find Dragon in it.

"Nic baby! Mama, where are you?" I hear Dragon call out in the distance.

I want to speak up, but I can't. I figure I'm dreaming, but I shake my head to try and figure out exactly what is going on.

"Fuck!" That came from Irish. He sounds panicked, so maybe I'm not dreaming.

Irish starts to back away towards the rock where Dani and I

first hid. I try and steady myself and lurch up to stand, but sway dangerously almost falling back down. At least my vision seems to be clearing a little.

"Dragon," I call out or whisper, I can't be sure, so I try again. "Dragon!" Shit, was that any louder?

I hear Dragon running towards us now. I look back at Irish and he's still pointing the gun. I know instantly what he has planned.

Dragon just makes it into my vision before I run towards him, trying to shield him.

Dragon

My world stops, it fucking stops. I see Nicole falling towards me and she's covered in blood. She doesn't have a shirt on, there are scratches all over her body and her face is swollen and red. She's saying my name, but it's garbled and I try to catch her before she falls. She's in my arms, but before my heart can calm....

Two shots, two fucking shots, as the explosion of the gunfire rings out, as if in slow motion. Bang...bang...and with each horrendous noise my woman's body jerks. I scream out in agony because it feels as if my fucking heart is being ripped from my chest.

I hear more gun shots but they are coming from behind me. My men are here, but I can't feel relief.

I fall to the ground holding my woman. I look up to see Irish, MY FUCKING BROTHER, holding the gun that just shot my woman. He's on his knees now, bleeding himself, since one of Crush's shots hit him in the arm. Bull has him down and slams his fist into the side of his head.

I look back at Nicole afraid to move. I can feel the blood on my hands where I'm holding her. I lean back to look at her face and her blue eyes are watching me. They're dazed and dilated, but she's staring at me with a smile. She has a fucking smile on her lips.

I bring my hand up and shakily hold the side of her face. The blood instantly smears on her hair and I hate it. It looks wrong. An obscenity on the only beautiful thing I've ever known.

"I knew you'd come," she whispers weakly, and it's all I can do to keep from screaming out at the pain gathering inside of me.

"I'm here Mama. You have to hold on for me," I say, petting her hair gently. I look over at Crush. "Get the ATV here NOW! Use the two-way and have Doc meet us at the bottom."

"Dragon…I love you."

"Mama, stop that shit. You're going to be fine. Just hold on and I'll have you fixed up in no time."

"Love you…"

"If you do, then you promise me you'll fight to stay with me. Do you hear me Nicole? You fight that shit and hold on. You got me?"

She grimaces and it guts me all over again to know she's hurting, but I will my strength into her.

"I…don't think…I…"

"Fuck that shit, you listen to me Mama. I told you that you were mine. You aren't getting away this easily. You asked for me and you got me. Now you have to stick around for the ride. Promise me Mama, we got a fucking life together to live. If you love me, you don't give up on that."

"Okay, Dragon," she says, and I reach down and kiss her on the forehead.

"Shit, hurry!" I look up at Bull and the pity in his eyes almost does me in. Nicole's head falls to the side at a weird angle. Her eyes are closed and for a second my heart stops.

She's slipping away from me. Tears fall from my own eyes and I don't think I've ever fucking cried in my life. Before Nicole I had nothing I really gave a fuck about, and if she's gone

I don't want to keep going either. She made the world bearable, when I didn't even know how damned miserable it really was.

"Oh God Mama, don't leave me. Don't leave me here without you," I say into her ear, holding her closer.

I hear Crush and he somehow has got the ATV's up here. I don't fucking know how he did it, but I'm so glad. Somehow Frog and I make it to the bottom of the hill. Crush took a separate vehicle and collected Dani. I couldn't worry about any of that. Nicole was still breathing, but there was so much blood. I used my shirt to hold pressure on her wound, but it was soaked by the time we made it to the bottom. Doc took over and I'm not sure what he did, but somehow he slowed the bleeding down. He had put a portable oxygen mask on her to help her breathing, but my heart wouldn't stop jumping.

I'm standing, watching Doc work on her and she looks so pale and lifeless. Her words replay in my head.

I love you Dragon. I love you Dragon.

It's like some fucked up song I have to keep listening to and can't turn off. I'm holding her hand and kissing the top of her head. My coat is covering her as best it can, while still allowing Doc room to work. There's so much blood, on her, me and Doc. I'm losing her. I had her and I didn't take care of her. I didn't keep her safe. She was precious and I let her be torn away from me. I should have known there were traitors in my club and I should have protected her more.

The ambulance pulls up and the medics come over to put her on the gurney. They put her in the ambulance and I'm just about to get in when the monitor they hook her up to flat lines. IT FUCKING FLAT LINES!

I try to get into the ambulance and my men grab me to hold

me back. The medics are working furiously on her and one is holding paddles above her heart.

"Mama, you hold the fuck on! You promised me! Don't you leave me woman or I swear to fucking Christ I will find a way to follow you and drag your fucking ass back here! NICOLE!!"

My body is shaking, I know I'm crying and I don't give one good fuck if that makes me a pussy to my men. I don't even fucking want them around right now. It's because of my motherfucking club, that my woman… Jesus Christ, she can't die. I reach up and grab my head, pulling my neck down so I'm staring at the ground and the tears fall and hit my muddy boots. How the fuck did this happen? How did I not know Irish was involved? How could I trust him with my woman?

Dragon

We made it to St. Lutheran's Hospital. We had been here for three fucking hours. Three hours of the most perverse hell I had ever been in. Crusher, Gunner, Freak and Striker were all here with me the whole time. Bull had just made it in, after delivering Irish to the Shed and having Frog and Nailer watching over him. I couldn't deal with that motherfucker yet, but I would soon enough.

My woman had barely been hanging onto life when we got her to the hospital. I lied and told them I was her fiancé and only living relative to give them permission to do emergency surgery.

They rolled her away from me and I haven't seen her since. If she died… fuck I couldn't even think that word.

"Mr. West?" A doctor comes out into the waiting area, and looks around.

I stand up immediately, my damn legs felt like rubber. I hear my brothers all come to stand behind me. I'm not sure how I feel about that right now. Can I trust them? Are there more traitors like Irish? I can't let my mind go there, not right now. My focus has to be on my woman.

"I'm Dra… Mr. West," I call out.

"Mr. West your fiancé is still holding on. The next forty-eight hours are critical. She went into shock and she's lost a lot of blood. A weaker person wouldn't have survived that. She was shot twice on top of that. The one to her side hip will cause her some discomfort from here out, but all things considered, not much else. The real damage came from the shot she received in her kidney. The organ was hit and with the amount of blood loss and the trajectory of the bullet, the damage was massive. The kidney was a total loss."

I want to sink to my knees, but I don't. I wait for more from him, and try to concentrate on the fact that my woman is still holding on.

"Will she..." I clear my throat. "Will she live?"

"She has a good chance, yes. As I said, the next forty-eight hours are critical. We'll monitor her and watch her closely. She'll be getting plasma and fluids through the night. Her vitals are weak but steady."

"I want to see her." He looks around at me and my brothers.

"She's in intensive care. I'm sorry, but we only allow certain visiting hours on that floor."

"Listen Doctor, I can appreciate rules, but that is my woman lying in there by herself. You told me the next forty-eight hours are critical and there is no way in hell that I am not going to be by her side every damn one of those hours. She's my woman and no one will keep me from her. Are we clear?"

The doctor swallowed and his eyes moved over the men behind me and finally rested back on mine.

"I will not allow any disruption. The first commotion, I will have security escort you out and bar you from the premises."

"Fair enough." Like fuck he would.

He nodded and reluctantly said with his back to me, "Follow me."

She looks so weak lying in the bed. Her skin is pale and washed out. She blends in with the stark white of the hospital sheets. I sit in the chair beside her and immediately wrap my hand around hers.

I have always enjoyed the differences of our color when we are together. The deep contrast is like something we shared, polar opposites attracting and clinging tight. Tonight her color is way too pale. She's still beautiful, but she is so cold to the touch.

I bring my hand up and shakily touch her hair. A nurse had obviously cleaned her hair and body. Even so, the horrible sight of her blood is engrained in my brain and I can still see it.

"I'm here Mama. I told you, you got me now. I'll always be here for you. You just got to live up to your end of the deal woman and wake up. I need you Mama. I fucking need you," I whisper close to her ear.

"I need you, Mama." I repeat that on and off willing her to listen to it. I need her to know it, because I know if she hears it, she will do whatever she has to do, to come back to me. Eventually, I lay my forehead down on our hands and just soak in being close to her.

Nicole

I feel so cold and it's dark. I can't seem to pull myself out. Did I fall into a hole? Everything just seems so hazy and I can't grasp anything around me. I hear him though, off in the background, I hear Dragon telling me he needs me and I panic. What's wrong? I doubt Dragon has ever admitted to anyone he needed them. My lips feel so dry and I lick them to try and speak.

"Dragon?" I croak. I seriously croaked. I don't know what's wrong with my voice, but my whole body feels weird.

"Nicole?" Dragon speaks back in a voice I had never heard from him before.

"I need you to…" I try to tell him, because I can feel the darkness begin to pull me back under.

When I come back through, I manage to open my eyes this time. My head feels like it has been hit over and over by a sledge hammer, and my body feels just as bad. I look around the dark room and see Dragon lying asleep in the chair beside my bed.

"Dragon?"

His body jerks awake instantly.

"Mama," he says, as his mouth comes down and he kisses my forehead gently.

"Thirsty…" I croak and he immediately reaches over to a table and gets me a drink from a glass there. It seems to take all my energy just to suck out of the straw.

"What happened?"

"Don't you remember Mama?"

"No, but I feel like I've been ran over by a Mack Truck. Was I in an accident?"

His big hand comes down and caresses the side of my face. His eyes are so deep and intense I can't look away, and there is moisture there too. I feel like I am missing something big here.

"Something like that, but you're going to be okay Mama and that's all that matters."

"You look tired."

"Yeah well, when my woman gets shot I tend to not get any sleep."

"Shot...oh God Dragon, Irish..."

"Shh...it's all okay now Mama but when the police ask you questions, I need you to tell them you don't know who kidnapped you. That you have no idea who they are and you've never seen them before. Can you do that for me?"

"Dragon..."

"I'll explain later, I promise."

"Dragon...Dani?"

"She's going to be okay, Mama. She's already been released. She's at the club where we can watch over her."

"She's released? How long? How long have I been here?" I ask, feeling unease move through me.

"A week."

"A week?" I croak.

"You developed an infection and were in a coma for a while, but you kept fighting and holding on. That's all that matters. Jesus Mama, I'm so glad you've come back to me."

I gave him a weak smile, feeling something close to happiness spread through me. He cared.

"Well! I see your fiancé has decided to wake up and join us Mr. West," an older nurse says, walking into the room. I look over at Dragon and mouth, "Fiancé?"

He grins big and that 'close to happiness' I felt earlier explodes beyond measure.

"We were beginning to wonder about you young lady."

"Sorry," I tell her, tightening my hand around Dragon's.

"Do you need anything?"

"A bath?" I really wanted one, I felt horribly grungy.

"We can't do that right now, but we'll see about getting you cleaned up in a bit. There are some detectives wanting to talk with you. I'm supposed to call them when you are able to talk."

"She's just..."

I pulled on Dragon's hand to stop him from going on.

"Sure, go ahead."

"I want a doctor checking her out first."

The nurse looked back at Dragon with a frown, but nodded her head in agreement.

"Mama....," he started, but I interrupted him.

"It'll be fine Dragon and the sooner we get rid of them the better. Shit! What happened to the clothes I was wearing?" I ask in a panic as I remember more of what had transpired.

"There wasn't much left of them, the doctors cut them up and the police took it with them for processing."

"Fuck! Dragon we have to..."

"Calm down Nic, you can't get upset and besides we had a cleaner get rid of any..."

"Dragon no, there was a SD card in my pocket! It had pictures of you and some man in a tub and the... shit we can't let the police find it..."

"I got it Mama, Doc found it when he was working on you. Mama we need to talk…"

"Not now. If you want you can tell me later. But not here around so many…"

Dragon looked at me strangely but nodded.

"You're mine," he said, almost in disbelief.

"And you're mine," I said, hoping he understood.

He bent down and kissed my lips gently, and then whispers in my ear.

"Forever Mama. Forever."

I wasn't sure how it happened, how our mixed up, fast paced relationship somehow transpired into forever, but I fully believed in it. Whatever this was between Dragon and me, it was indeed, forever.

Dragon

She unmans me. Just when I think I have her figured out, Nicole does something to completely blow me out of the water. Will I ever be prepared for her? I'm starting to think not and I'm okay with that, to a point.

I watched her calmly tell the investigating detectives she had no memory of what happened. She was hit from behind and from there it was all blank. The doctors could only confirm she had been hit and had suffered a concussion and amnesia could occur after a traumatic injury. I just shook my head, but inside, fuck inside, I felt raw at times. She was completely cemented in me now. She had been before, but now with every day that passes, I am completely and irrevocably wrapped up in her.

It wasn't just me either. My men had completely adopted Nic as one of our own. Maybe it was because she had been hurt by Irish? Maybe it's the way she took two bullets to save me? Maybe it was the way she put her life on the line to protect me and to cover for the club? I don't know. Maybe they are just as dazzled by her as I am. I couldn't explain it, but it just gave me another reason to believe she is the one.

I smile as I see her in action now. It's her first night home and the club is partying. Even the Twinkies are on their best behavior. Nicole cemented her place in this club by taking on Tasha.

Tasha is in the corner talking with a couple of the prospects, avoiding my woman at all costs. She has more brains than I gave her credit for.

Nicole is at the bar talking to the new prospect, Six. I don't know the kid that well yet, but he has promise. We hired him in as a bartender to take that fucker Irish's place.

Crush passes a drink to my woman. She takes it, walks over to me with a sassy grin and I pull her onto my lap.

"What are you drinking baby?" I ask figuring her, Crusher and Six were up to something since they all have shit eating grins on their faces.

"It's a new drink Six fixed for me," she says, looking back sideways at me and kissing me lightly on the lips. She turns back around and takes another sip of her drink. My fingers comb through her hair, my other hand on her thigh. This is the best I've felt in nearly a month. That's how long my woman has been in the hospital away from me. Three long fucking torturous weeks and finally she's home in my arms where she belongs.

Her girl Dani was back in the kitchen. She wasn't adjusting very well at all to living at the club. I wasn't sure what her story was, but since the scene at the house, she had been a different woman, showing none of the fire or life she had earlier. I knew Nicole was worried about her, but Dani so far wouldn't even talk to her.

"Did you hear me?" she asks.

"Sorry Mama was busy enjoying having you in my arms again." She leans back against me with a happy sigh. "What'd you say?"

"I wanted to know if you were curious as to what my new drink is called."

"Okay Mama, I'll bite."

"I hope so," she chimes in. I shake my head and slap her gently on the thigh.

"Behave woman, you know what the doctor said."

"That doctor is an agent of the devil. No sex for two weeks? I'll grow cobwebs! Dragon did you get a look at the old geezer? He probably hasn't ever had good sex in his life! He obviously doesn't realize sex releases endorphins that boost your immune system."

"Is that a fact?"

"Totally! Why, sex can speed up the healing process by over one hundred and twenty per cent."

"I see you've been doing your research."

"I totally have."

"Too bad."

"It is?" she asks, confused.

I lean in close to whisper in her ear. "Yeah Mama, because I'm not giving you my cock until I'm sure you're completely healed."

"You suck."

"I thought you liked it when I sucked on you," I said, kissing the back of her neck.

"Hey there's an idea."

"What's that Mama?" I ask holding her and just breathing in her scent.

She turns to the side and looks at me and right away I can see I'm in trouble.

"I could suck you off and let you come down my throat. That way even if I can't come, I can still taste you."

Fuck. She's trying to kill me, or make me come in my jeans—hell maybe both.

"Not going to happen Mama. I'm not getting off until I can make sure you do too."

"Meanie," she says, sticking her bottom lip out in a pout.

"Now what are you drinking?" I'm trying to will my raging hard-on back under control. It's going to be a long month. I haven't told Nicole, but even though the Doctor said she could have sexual relations after two weeks, I'm not going to touch her for at least a month. I will not put her life in jeopardy. It already bothers me that because of my failure to protect her, she's walking around with only one kidney. If something were to happen to it...to her...

"Crush said it was a drink made especially for me," she said, proudly finishing it off with a smack of her lips.

"And why is that Mama?" I ask intrigued now.

"It's called, Dragon's Balls!" she says, with a sparkle in those damn blue eyes. I look up at Crush and Six who are laughing their asses off, obviously knowing she's told me. I flip them off and then shift her gently so I can pick her up and start walking back to our room.

"Did I mention you have a tendency to pick me up and carry me a lot?"

"I seem to recall that."

"Just checking," she says, resting her head on my shoulder.

I stand her in front of our bed and go back to lock our door.

"God I'm glad you're home."

"What has happened to my gruff Dragon?" she asks, watching as I begin undressing her.

I unbutton her shirt first, my eyes holding hers.

"You saved him," I said, pulling the shirt from her arms and tossing it on the floor.

"I think he saved me."

"He was the idiot who let you get hurt," I say honestly, and wait while she kicks her shoes off and I do the same.

"He came and saved me," she argued. I pull her jogging pants and underwear down gently, knowing she's still sore from the surgery.

I turn her around and kiss her back while I unhook her bra. Once I have it unhooked I lean down and kiss the scar from her surgery which is longer than it would have been normally because of the damage. Then I kiss the bullet wound off to the side of the incision. Finally, I kiss the bullet wound on her thigh.

"Is it ugly Dragon?" she asks, her voice trembling. I gently lay her on the bed and then climb in beside her, pulling the covers up over us.

She holds me close, her head on my chest and this might be the first time I've breathed easily since she was hurt.

"It's beautiful Mama. Everything about you is beautiful to me."

"It's a horrendous scar, they both are Dragon! There's no way it can be beautiful."

"It is to me. It's proof to me that somehow despite everything, you've found a way to love my fucked up ass."

"I love everything about you."

"I've got scars, inside and out Mama. Do they make you care about me any less?"

"No way!"

"You heard the kind of filth I was born from, the kind of person I am. How I even got my damn name. Does that change the way you feel about me?"

"No. I love your name. I've been to Detroit you know. Do

you know what I've always found amazing?"

"What's that Mama?" I ask, my hands finding her hair again and twirling it around my fingers.

"People only see the broken sad parts of Detroit, but if you look closer? If you take the time to investigate and see everything it has to offer, the truth is it is an amazing and beautiful city. So I think the name fits you perfectly."

Fuck. She's done it again. I have so many emotions welling up inside of me that I'm not sure I'll be able to choke them back down.

"Do you love me Dragon?" she asks and she sounds so insecure, but hell I don't know how to answer that.

"I don't know what love is Nicole."

"Oh," she says so quietly into the empty room. I can hear the disappointment in her voice and it makes me feel like shit. I don't want to lie, but I honestly don't know what that shit is.

"Fuck baby. Don't you get it? Have you seen how a stone breaks and shatters with the ring of a sledge hammer? Pieces just bust into so many different size chunks you'll never get them back together? I'm like a goddamned tombstone that has been broken into so many fucking pieces that some turn to dust. I've never been scared before in my life, but you scare me. You break me woman, you fucking break me apart. I failed to keep you safe and I can't let that shit happen again. So I ask myself how the fuck do I keep you safe when you leave me so damned defenseless."

"That sounds a little bit like love to me," she responds, so damned hopeful that another layer of ice I used to keep wrapped around me falls away.

"Mama, how am I supposed to say I love you? I don't know

what that is. Hell mama, I crave you. I fucking need you so bad I can't breathe unless you're close by. If that's love then fucking sign me up, I'm there as long as you're with me. God baby girl... I need you with me," I say closing my eyes, trying to still the pain I feel that I might have hurt her.

I feel moisture falling onto my chest and look down to see my woman wiping her eyes. Shit I made it worse.

"Mama, I'm sorry..."

"I love you so much Dragon, everything about you is perfect for me."

I swallow down more words. I'm longing to open up to her, but I can't. That's not fair to my woman, but I need to regroup.

"Go to sleep Mama. It's been a busy day for you. Me and the boys need to go take care of some things tomorrow."

"I'm sorry Dragon. I know how much it hurts you and even if you don't want to talk about it, I know what you're doing."

"Nicole, don't ask me to change. The club has a code and I live by a code. I love you, but if I let one fucker get away with shit like this, then a mountain of..."

"I'm not asking for anything Dragon, I'm not stupid. I'm just asking that you don't lie to me about things or keep them from me. This is who you are, and I've seen it up close even if you never meant for me to, and I'm still here."

"I can't always share what's going on with you Nicole and that's as much for your safety as anything else."

"When I ask, you will tell me what you can."

I swallow, wondering if this will bite me in the fucking ass.

"I'll try."

"Good enough."

"Are you done busting my balls now? Can we go to sleep?"

"Since you won't give me cock, I guess we might as well."

"God I had no idea what I was in for when I claimed you," I said with a smile, kissing the top of her head.

"Night sweetheart," she whispers.

I lay there listening as her breathing evens out and she drifts to sleep.

Nicole

He's killing me. It's been four weeks since I've been out of the hospital and he still won't have sex with me. I know he wants it, he's denying himself as much as he is me. It's driving me crazy. He won't listen to reason, even when I had the doctor talk to him personally.

Still, tonight was the night. How did I know this? I had a surprise planned for him. I had Dani and Bull taking me out during the day while Dragon's been away dealing with Irish. I hadn't asked, but I knew whatever was going on was extra hard on him.

I hated my scars and I especially hated that they would be a reminder to Dragon of a betrayal by his brother. I hated they made him feel like he let me down. So I decided to do something drastic. In the past two weeks I had gotten an outline started, going from the first gunshot wound that covered my entire right ass cheek, all along my incision and up my back wrapping around my arm. It was a gigantic Dragon tattoo and I loved it. I couldn't wait to get it colored in. Today was the first appointment for the shading and I had also put a smaller tattoo on my neck which was a dragon's wing that had the word 'mine' woven into the scales. The dragon's fire moved up my back over my left shoulder and ended with a plume of smoke on the top of my hand that said 'Property of Dragon' in it. Now, I may have gone overboard and I was nervous as heck. I was also thankful

Dragon had been keeping late nights at the Shed. Though the reason why sucked, it had helped me be able to keep my secret a secret.

Tonight was New Year's Eve, and because of everything that had been going on we had completely missed Christmas. So I had extra celebrating to do. Dragon doesn't know it yet, but he will be giving me what I want.

The club is packed, since some of the sister chapter from Ohio were in visiting. I'm wearing a dark red sweater dress that ends just above my knees. It has a turtle neck collar and covered every part of me. I had my black, high heel, fuck me boots on and my hair was starting to go back to light blonde because I had stopped adding the chestnut. I looked hot. I know I did. I was bummed Dani wouldn't be here tonight to see me in action, but she was spending New Years with her brother.

I watch Dragon from the bar. His eyes are on me. I grab my drink that Six slides over with a wink and take a drink, lifting the cherry out and sucking on it. It's a lame flirt, and horribly obvious, but it's working so I climb on the stool, allowing my dress to ride up my thigh.

"You're playing with fire girl," Crusher said laughing.

"I hope so."

"Lucky Bastard doesn't know what's about to hit him does he?"

I look back over at Dragon and he's watching us so closely I practically feel the heat from his gaze.

"I hope not," I grin and we both laugh as I take another drink.

"Get the fuck away from my woman," Dragon barks, catching me off guard. Damn he moves fast.

Breaking **DRAGON**

I watch as Crush salutes me and walks off shaking his head.

"That was kind of rude."

"He was trying to look at your ass. Pull your dress down woman."

"Dragon, don't be silly it's covering everything. If it wasn't I'd be in trouble."

"Damn right, because I'd tan your ass."

"You're always threatening that, but seems like you haven't delivered very often. Still, it's not what I meant. I meant I'm not wearing any underwear."

"What the fuck?" he growls grabbing my arm and pulling me towards him.

I lean up to whisper in his ear so only he can hear me, though I'm pretty sure everyone knows by this point what I am doing.

"I'm horny, Dragon. I need your cock. I thought if I went commando, we wouldn't waste time and you could just bend me over the bar and fuck me hard."

"Nicole...," he groans out.

My tongue darts out to twirl into his ear.

"Please Dragon take me to our room and fuck me so hard I scream loud enough everyone knows how good you're giving it to me."

I reach up letting the long loose sleeve of my dress ride up and reveal my tattoo to him. He grabs my arm and looks at it. When he reads 'Property of Dragon', I feel his hand shake. His thumb traces it and his eyes go deep, intense black.

He grabs my drink off the counter and throws it across the bar to the glasses on a shelf. Several shatter and the clatter of glass is so loud immediately the crowd quiets.

"OUT!" he orders.

I don't think they understand what he is saying because they are all just kind of watching him. I glance around and see several mouths drop open. Dragon's always so self-contained, that had I not been getting glimpses of this new Dragon, I wouldn't have believed it either.

"I said get the fuck out! Crush you guard the front door and if anyone sets their ass in here until I'm finished fucking my woman I will kill them. You understand?"

"Yes sir, Bossman. You heard the man! The party moves outside!"

I stare at Dragon while all around us people run to get out of Dragon's way. My nipples are hard and I'm already so wet I can feel the moisture on my thighs.

He steps away from me and starts stripping while I watch. He doesn't do it slow either, and is completely undressed in no time. Then he's staring at me.

"Who told you it was okay for you to mark that skin up Nicole?"

"Don't you like it?" Worried now because of what he has yet to see.

"Fuck yeah, but I don't like the idea of some fucker touching your body without me there Nicole. You get a spanking for that."

Umm...yikes, now I am nervous about revealing the rest of it to him.

"It was a woman. Bull wouldn't let Lee work on me."

"Well it appears at least one of my men still has his brains. Time to strip, Mama and don't you dare act like you don't want this, after you begged me for it," he says stroking his cock slowly, his eyes never leaving mine. God he looks so damned good, just like that.

His hand moving over his huge cock is the hottest thing I've ever seen in my life. I can feel the heat move through my body. I can feel the wetness sliding down between my thighs. My legs grow weak. It's time and though I'm a little worried, I'm too turned on to resist. I bend down to start with my boots, figuring that would be easier.

"Leave the fucking boots on," he growls, still stroking his cock.

I lick my lips seeing the wet sticky drop on his cock's head and wishing I could taste it. I take a deep breath figuring I've delayed enough, grab my sweater dress and pull it over my head in one quick movement. His eyes grow hard and he's staring at the tattoo on my neck. I know he can only glimpse it from this angle. So I decide to bite the bullet.

"What the fuck did you…"

I turn around and face the bar, pull my hair to the side of my neck and over my shoulder so he can see the complete tattoo.

He makes a sound like an animal. His hand goes first to my thigh which is the beginning of the tattoo and travels over my ass and up my back.

He grabs my hair and yanks my head back and growls in my ear again.

"Lean over this fucking bar and hold the fuck on because I'm going to wear your sweet little pussy out."

"God yes," I moan bending over, spacing my legs apart to make room for him. My hands grasp the bar and I hold on tight. I know what's coming; I ache for what's coming.

"That's it Mama. I hope you're ready for me because I'm not waiting."

"I'm ready Dragon, I'm more than…"

I scream out in pleasure as he slams into me. The first stroke is hard and powerful as he sinks all the way in. I feel his balls slap against me. It takes my breath away. It has been a while, and the feel of him is amazing but extremely tight. I feel so full it's on the verge of painful but in a very good way.

He grabs my hair again pulling my head back as he leans over me, his strokes slower and smoother now, but just as powerful.

"Is this what you wanted Nicole? Did you need me to fuck you so hard you'll walk crooked for a week?"

"Yes…"

"You belong to me. My mark all over your body, I know what you've given me and you're not fucking getting it back, you hear me Mama? You're mine."

"Forever," I gasp, as he slams home again and again.

"Play with your clit Mama. Do it, I'm close and I want to feel you explode all over my cock before I blow."

I do as he orders, but I'm so close that with just one touch, I shoot off into the stars. It's so intense I'm barely lucid when he joins me just moments later.

* * *

It's been a few hours, we've made it to our room, but I can still hear the party outside. They are probably afraid to come back in and the thought of it makes me giggle.

"What's so funny Mama?"

"I'm happy."

He leans down and kisses me, his tongue caressing mine

slow and soft and sucking on it gently. It lacks the ferocity usually involved in our lovemaking, but instead it feels sweet and gentle like he is savoring our connection. Maybe that's just what I'm feeling, either way, it is divine.

"I love you, Detroit 'Dragon' West."

"I love you too, Mama, down to the marrow in my bones. Forever."

Holy fuck!

I get the words from him that I thought I would never hear. I cry like a big baby. I can't help it. I knew he did, well mostly. Yet, to actually hear him say the words, does something to me I wasn't expecting at all.

"Forever," I sniffle and cry harder.

Dragon sits up in bed and gathers me in his arms. His hand strokes softly in my hair and his presence warms me all the way through.

"Forever," he whispers while he holds me close.

We don't say anything else, but then again, nothing needs to be said. Nothing at all. In this moment, I know without a shadow of a doubt, I am in the one place in this world I was born to be. Dragon's arms.

Dragon

I stand looking at what is left of a man I used to respect. There's not much there anymore and in the month we have been interrogating him, I had only learned bits and pieces.

The man responsible for the mayhem in my club, and ultimately nearly killing my woman is an unknown shadow and I don't like that shit one bit.

Irish had caved enough to tell me it all somehow linked in with Dancer, and the two of us pissing off the wrong people. At least I had a direction to look into now.

Irish was pretty unrecognizable. We branded his tats off, the ones concerning the club at least. Freak had been working on him with a razor. The word traitor written across Irish's chest was an extra special touch. Now he was in an oil drum. I can't bring myself to let the soup finish him off like we had with Twist. I am going to be slightly more humane.

"I'll see you in hell brother," I tell him as I aim my 45 at his dick and then empty the chamber.

I look over at Bull.

"After he has breathed his last, go ahead and add the stew. When you're done, dump him and blast the fucker."

We were going to pour Irish in the old abandoned deep mine. We'd have to pour him because with the stew, there won't be anything left of him. Irish had a fear of being underground, so I felt it was poetic justice.

I turn and walk away. I have a woman to get back to. I also need Freak to start digging up information on this Phoenix. If this fucker thought he'd play with my club, he had another think coming. I'd make him sorry he ever tried.

I pull out my cell phone as I make it to the SUV.

"I need Dancer out like yesterday. Quit dragging your ass and make it happen Eagle or I'll find someone who can, you feel me?"

His voice drones on.

"No more excuses. Do it. I need my brother out of that shit hole like yesterday. You feel me?"

I don't give him time to respond. I hang up and head back to the club. It's time I start circling the wagons. I expect to know who the fuck thought he could toy with me by the end of the night and when I do, he will know who in the hell the Savage MC was and how the fuck we got our name.

Read on for a sneak peek
into the next installment of the
Savage MC Series: Saving Dancer

Prologue

'The Nightmare'
Dancer

It's dark, pitch black. I can feel the hands holding me down. The laughter fades into the background as my heart accelerates and beats out of control. The sound drums in my ears and a fine sweat pops out over my body. I slam my head back with all of my might. I choke on the fear and I despise myself for it. The fear makes me feel weak and I have never been weak in my life.

The back of my head connects with some motherfucker and the feeling of blood smears against my bald head. I slam my head again hoping I can kill the son of a bitch.

I scream out as dirty hands try to clamp over my mouth. I twist and turn until I can get just enough of the hand in my mouth to bite down and tear. I do it with an angry scream. There's a moment of disappointment when I can't manage to tear the finger off with just the force of my teeth.

Still, it's enough to get room so I can throw an elbow into the son of a bitch's stomach that's been helping to restrain me. There are four of the motherfuckers holding me, three now that the guy behind me let go. I hope I at least killed him. I will kill them all though.

I will tear them apart piece by piece. That is the last clear thought I have before a large silver flash comes at me.

I feel the impact of the pipe against the side of my head. I hear that voice. The voice I hate so much it continuously churns in my gut and eats at me from the inside out.

"Got something for you pretty boy," the voice says, as the darkness encloses around me.

It was six words. It was six words that would bring death, six words that would change me forever, six words that would destroy me and start my path through hell.

Chapter 1

Dancer

It's dark but not night, that much I know. The heavy, foam-backed curtains are pulled tight over the window and a small sliver of light is allowed to shine where the two panels meet. There is a pounding behind my eyes and a cold sweaty mist covers my body. My head is swimming and I close my eyes against the gut clenching nausea that slams me.

Waking up like this is nothing new. It's the normal, my new fucked up normal. The room smells of smoke, cheap whiskey, perfumed whores, and sex. Fuck I've stuck my dick in so much loose pussy in the last week, the damn thing smells like week old tuna.

I rub my head over the short stubble on my head. In the week I've been out of the joint, I've started letting it grow. In prison it was better to let the Screws keep it cut. There are just too many fucking bugs in that damn hell hole. I'm not sure if I'll cut it again. Anything different from being there is better. I never want anything to remind me of being in that shit hole again.

I push bodies off of me and move to the edge of the bed. The two chicks in the bed should have got their skanky asses out last night. One of them grumbles in complaint but she rolls her ass over on her girlfriend and goes back out. When I look over at the lily white ass sticking up in the air my hand automatically goes down to my dick and stretches it. Damn thing doesn't take the hint though. If anything, it seems to want to crawl inside of my balls and hide. It's a shame because it's a damn fine ass, but what the fuck ever. I stand up and the world spins as my body tilts too far to the left. I right myself and walk towards the bathroom, cursing when my bare feet kick one of the empty liquor bottles on the floor.

Fuck that hurt. I lean over to pick the bottle up and the world tilts again. This time I overestimate my coordination and fall. I maneuver at the last minute and land on my side instead of my motherfucking head. I lay there a minute looking up at the darkness. It hurts to breathe, not really from the fall. Hell it's hurt to breathe for so long I can't remember when it was ever any other way. Why the fuck I couldn't just swallow a bullet and get it over with, I don't even know. I'm so fucking tired of fighting it all. So fucking tired…

"Dancer open up man!" The hard knocking on the front of the old hotel door jumps with the vibration of the pounding it receives.

My head goes down, both hands raking over it again. Fuck, I don't want my brothers here. Why couldn't they just leave me alone? I told them fuckers that I….

"Dancer open this fucking door or I'm kicking it in!" Crusher yells, as he pounds the damn door again. I wince at the pain the noise brings.

I start getting up. I may not have had shit to do with my brothers since I got out of the joint, but I know he's not going to give up. Before I can right myself enough to pick my ass up off of the floor, the door slams open and bounces off the wall with a huge cracking noise. I wince at the pain that brings and close my eyes against the glaring light that is now in the room.

"Fucking hell! Close the damn-fucking-son-of-a-bitching

door," I groan, not bothering to turn around and look at Crusher. It's better to keep my back against the light. Fucking shit is bright enough like this.

"Oh God."

I turn my head against my will when I hear that voice. I know that voice, that voice is imbedded in my brain, my motherfucking black soul. I'm going to fucking rip Crusher's head off. My eyes lock with the one person in this world I never expected nor wanted to lay eyes on again.

"What the fuck are you doing here?"

She jerks back like I just physically hit her. I've never hit a woman in my life, but if I was going to start, it would be with her ass.

"Hi, Jacob," she whispers into the room and it fucking makes me want to scream and roar at her. I don't want her here. I don't want to see her, I don't want to deal with her and I sure as fuck don't want to hear that sweet ass voice saying my fucking name. She's poison. She's a fucking knife to the gut that repeatedly stabs. She's the reason my head is all fucked up, that my life is all fucked up and most of all she is the reason I want to fucking swallow a bullet.

"GET THE FUCK OUT OF THIS ROOM!" I roar pulling myself up and charging towards her.

She gasps and backs up against the hotel door. I'm almost to her. I don't know what I'm going to do when I reach her. I really don't. I might even strangle the life out of her. I know I will push her out of my fucking room, out of my space, out of my life. I know it. In the end the point is moot though because Crusher jumps in front of me and stops me from reaching her.

We're pretty evenly matched, but if I had been sober he

wouldn't have been able to stop me. As it is, he contains me and looks over his shoulder.

"Carrie, wait for me by my bike Darlin'."

"Okay Alexander," she whispers, and gives me one more tortured look.

Her green eyes are filled with tears, but I don't fucking care. Her and her tears can rot in fucking hell. I think that and then my mind shifts back. Alexander? What the fuck?

"Are you sinking your dick in that cunt?" I ask in disgust, pushing away from Crusher.

"Jesus H. Christ Dance, what the fuck? You smell like a damned gutter," Crusher says, his face curled in disgust.

The bitches from last night are sitting up in bed looking at me and Crusher and it pisses me off. I told them to be gone by morning. I don't even know why I keep trying to bury myself in pussy. It's not working anyway and I sure as fuck don't want them around after.

"Get dressed and get the fuck out!" I growl and walk towards the small shower.

"If you're going to wait around till I get out, make sure those bitches leave," I order Crusher.

"Dance, man…"

"And you sure as fuck better keep that gash you came with outside."

I make it to the door before the crash is heard. I turn to look and Crusher has taken my empty liquor bottle and smashed the old mirror hanging on the wall opposite of the bed. Fuck I had been enjoying that mirror. That thought freezes in my mind as I look at my brother. His body is rigid with anger and gone is the laid back country ol' shucks cocky vibe he normally has.

"Dance I'm warning you, lay off of Carrie. I know you're fucked up, but that woman don't deserve your wrath and she sure as fuck don't need your insults."

I want to say more to him, but truth is I don't give a fuck. The sooner I shower and talk to his ass, the sooner he'll leave and I can find a new bottle.

"Whatever, sorry I insulted your Twinkie of the month," I grumble and slam the door on his curse.

Saving Dancer (Savage MC Series, Book 2)
is now available on Amazon.

55791283R00130

Made in the USA
Lexington, KY
03 October 2016